IT HAD TO BE MASON

BEACHBREAK HIGH #1

EMILY LOWRY

Cover Photography by
ANYA BERKUT VIA CANVA PRO

ELEVENTH AVENUE
PUBLISHING

A THANK YOU FROM EMILY

I wanted to take a moment to say thank you to my readers —
without you, none of this would be possible.

I truly appreciate every single review, Instagram post and
blog shout-out that you have given me. Every email, message
and kind word from you has brightened my day, every time.
You are the true MVPs!

To my ARC team, thank you for your endless encourage-
ment and incredibly helpful feedback. I value each and every
one of you.

Now, to write my next love story. Stay tuned!

Lots of love always,

XO, Emily

ZOE

*I*f a boy was hot, I admired him from afar.

Under no circumstances would I ever, EVER, walk over and strike up a conversation. What would I even say? Hi, I'm that totally-not-creepy girl who's been accidentally following you through the grocery aisles, and sure, we've never met, but I know every social media account you have? And I follow them all?

No.

You did not do that with hot boys.

You especially did not do that on days where you were sweaty and gross — which was a frequent occurrence for me this summer.

Late August, the heat wave hit California. It was so hot that if you stood still for too long, the soles of your shoes melted. It was humid, too, so as soon as you stepped outside, you started to sweat, and your clothes stuck to you. That wasn't a huge problem for most of the girls in my dance class. They all wore skin tight yoga gear anyway, and sweat just made them look even more athletic and toned.

It was a problem for girls like me, who favored shapeless

t-shirts over crop tops and whose already unruly hair became an out of control frizzy mess when exposed to damp heat.

The t-shirt that I was wearing — a baggy old Cal Tech hand-me-down — was plastered unflatteringly to my body. Worse, it smelled... probably because I forgot to put on deodorant before dance class. I dug through my gym bag, hoping a little white stick of floral powers was hiding beneath my sweat pants or buried in my towel. No such luck.

I looked around the locker room. The rest of the girls had left before me, probably headed to the beach. I poked through a few of the open lockers, hoping someone had forgotten a can of spray deodorant. I didn't like the smell, but it was better than smelling like, well, me.

Foiled again.

Oh well, I'd just have to make sure I didn't run into anybody I knew.

Outside, blistering heat replaced the air-conditioning of the dance studio.

My shoulders sagged, my body melting into the pavement. It was only a fifteen-minute walk from the studio to my house, but I suspected I'd be a human puddle before I made it halfway. A smelly human puddle. Gross.

I thought about walking straight home, not taking my usual detour. I really did.

But even as the thought was crossing my mind, my legs were guiding me towards High Street. Towards Him. And yes, he gets a capital H.

On Saturday mornings, High Street was the place to go in Beachbreak if you wanted fancy coffee and a toasted bagel with smeared avocado and sun-dried tomato. It was also the place to go if you wanted to do some shopping. Vibrant, colorful stores practically popped up from between palm trees and park benches. There were bakeries and antique shops, cafés and music venues, restaurants and old school lounges. The stores were on one side of the street. On the other side?

Highline Beach. A long expanse of golden sand, crashing surf, and more people than I could count. Families built sand castles, seniors roasted like Thanksgiving turkeys, and surfers rode waves.

As awesome as High Street was, there was only one shop I was interested in this morning. Sand and Sun Board Games was nestled between a pair of palm trees. It had a blue awning that showed two chess pieces — a knight and the castle thing — having a sword fight. The expansive bay windows were open today, letting the fresh ocean air flow inside.

I slowed my pace. A nervous energy swam in my stomach, the same kind of nervous you feel when you're going up the first hill on a rollercoaster. I stopped by a park bench. I didn't want to be too close — I wanted to see Him, but I didn't want to risk Him seeing me. Today, I would admire from afar.

As I mentioned: girls like me didn't talk to guys who were hot.

Kevin Gibbons walked between the aisles of board games, his hands folded neatly behind his back. He was tall and skinny, his hair a mess of wild curls. His general body shape reminded me of a palm tree. But like, a hot palm tree. He bent over, plucked a board game off a shelf, then held it up to examine the back.

My heart skipped like it was doing jump rope. I'd had a crush on Kevin since forever. Nina, my best friend, had never understood it. She thought Kevin was — and I quote — boring and pretentious. I disagreed. Kevin was smart. Not that I'd ever talked to him.

Kevin put the board game back on the shelf.

While he was doing his job, I was imagining what would happen if he noticed me. We'd make eye contact from across the street. His eyes would do that cartoon thing where they literally transform into hearts and his jaw would drop. Then he'd wave me over. I'd look behind myself, thinking he must be waving at someone else. But no. He'd be waving to me. So I'd go over. And he'd be the perfect gentleman. And he'd—

Wait, what was that smell?

I scrunched my nose and looked around for the source. Hmm… no garbage cans nearby. It couldn't be… it wasn't me, was it? As casually as I could, I took a slight whiff of myself.

Oh.

Oh no.

I was the smell. The morning heat had done me no favors. It was good that Kevin hadn't spotted me.

He hadn't, right?

I checked.

A girl approached Sand and Sun Board Games. She was taller than me — but then again, wasn't everyone? — and her hair was so perfect I assumed she was immune to heat. She opened the door. Kevin greeted her, smiling. The sound of their words didn't carry across the street, but the tone of their voices did. Happy. Light-hearted. Joyful.

My eye twitched. She was just a customer. It wasn't a big deal, he was just helping a customer. That was all.

The girl said something. Kevin laughed, then guided her towards one shelf. He pointed to several board games. She nodded excitely, said something else, and Kevin laughed again.

But she probably wasn't actually funny, I decided. Kevin was just being a good salesman and laughing at her lame jokes so he could up his commission. Because he was smart. I nodded to myself. That was definitely all that was happening.

Ms. Not Actually Funny carried her board game to the cashier's desk and Kevin rang it through. He put the receipt in a bag, then grabbed one of the business cards and scribbled something on the back.

My jaw dropped. Was he giving her his number? "What the—"

Kevin and Ms. Not Actually Funny both turned in my direction.

Oh no. My voice was at it again, speaking out loud when I didn't mean to. Deft ninja that I was, I quickly stumble-dove behind the park bench, hoping that they didn't see me. I crossed my fingers. They would have to be idiots to have not seen me. Especially considering you could see under the park bench. So now I was probably the crazy girl who spoke out loud to herself then hid behind park benches.

Please, please don't have seen me. I leaned over to peak around the bench.

"Mommy, why is that lady weird?"

I whipped my head around.

The high-pitched voice belonged to a boy who was maybe four. His face was scrunched up like he was struggling his way through a puzzle. The boy's mom, who was carrying a Starbucks cup, glared at me.

I shrugged and laughed awkwardly, like it was a totally normal thing to hide behind park benches while spying at the store across the street.

The boy's lip quivered.

He wasn't seriously about to cry, was he?

"I don't like her," he said, clutching his mother's hand tightly.

His mom shot me another look of disgust and pulled him along.

The boy craned his head to stare at me as he walked away.

I opted to do the mature thing and stick my tongue out.

The boy's eyes went wide.

I scurried out from behind the park bench before I could get in more trouble. I risked a glance across the street.

The girl was walking away from the shop, her bag comfortably in her hand. She waved at Kevin. He waved back, then retreated inside the store. It was a completely natural, completely normal, interaction.

The exact opposite of sweating to death while you cowered across the street. I wanted to chase the girl down and ask her how she made everything look so natural?

Why was talking to Kevin so easy for everyone who wasn't me?

MASON

*L*ate summer football? You couldn't beat it. It was the time of year where everyone was optimistic about the upcoming season. Walk into any high school, ask any player, and they would tell you that this was the year they were going to state.

For Beachbreak High, things were shaping up nicely. I was confident in my skills as quarterback. We had a great defensive line. No one was injured yet, either. Plus, practicing under the California sun gave you a great tan. Girls loved dudes with a great tan.

And I loved girls. Which is why I had one waiting for me in the stands.

Meredith sat in the bleachers. Her hair was long, blonde, and wavy — like the ripples in beach sand. She wore a polka dot sundress, and currently, one of her hands was holding her hair, scrunching it up, and the other was holding her cell, taking a selfie. She pursed her lips and winked at the camera, then studied the picture before sending it off. I'd dated my fair share of Beachbreak girls, but Meredith had only ever shown an interest in college boys.

I was determined to change that.

Coach blew his whistle, signaling the end of the practice. While the rest of the boys headed to the locker room, I took off my helmet, sprayed my face with the water bottle, then casually messed my hair and strolled over.

I winked. "Is it hot out here, or is it just you?"

Meredith rolled her eyes. "How many girls have you used that line on?"

"You mean today?" I held out my fingers, pretending to count. "I think just you. Feel special?"

Meredith rolled her eyes again.

I had a habit of making girls roll their eyes.

"I got your text," she said. "So, I'm here. I assume this is important?"

Important? The reason I asked Meredith to meet me here couldn't be more important. I looked away and curled my fingers on the neck of my shoulder pads, letting water drip down the side of my face. I felt nervous.

"Homecoming," I said. "You and me. What do you say?"

Meredith blinked. "Are you... you're asking me?"

Was I missing something? She was single, I was single. She was the captain of the dance team, I was the captain of the football team. We'd been texting lately. And because of that, I'd thought she'd changed her stance on dating high school guys. I thought I was in.

"Are you not going?"

Meredith cleared her throat. She eyed me up and down.

I smirked. "Want me to give you a twirl?"

"Yes, but not in the way you think," Meredith said. She wasn't checking me out so much as she was studying me. Like she was looking for weaknesses.

I suddenly felt self-conscious.

"Homecoming is a big deal," Meredith said. "Especially for me. I'm the captain of the dance team. The Homecoming dance competition is important to me. I need to win. The captain of the dance team always does."

Where was she going with this?

She raised her eyebrows. "So? Can you?"

"Can I what?"

"Dance."

I scoffed. "I can dance."

Meredith crossed her arms. "Prove it. Dance right here."

Right here, right now? Most of the guys had gone into the locker room, but a few of the sophomore receivers were still throwing balls with the backup quarterback. "There's no music," I said.

"Just show me the steps," Meredith said. "Do a two-step."

I would've rather gotten sacked by a three-hundred-pound defensive tackle than danced in the middle of a field, by myself, to no music. Especially because I didn't know how to dance. But how hard could it be to do a two-step? If you believed the name, there were only two steps involved. I could fake my way through two steps.

I stuck my hands out, pretending they were on my invisible partner's hips. Then I stepped forward with my right foot twice, then my left foot twice.

Meredith covered her mouth to hide a laugh. "Not even close."

I laughed nervously. "It's not that big of a deal."

"To you," Meredith said. "But to anyone on the dance team, it is. I wanted to say yes, Mason. But I can't sacrifice winning the competition. I won't go to Homecoming with someone that can't dance."

I was getting rejected. My cheeks burned, my eyes stung. This was a completely new experience. But, if dance was important to her, then it had to be important to me. "I can learn."

Meredith checked her phone, then stood. "Good. And

when you learn, and you can prove it, let me know. Then maybe I'll say yes. If you're worth my time."

Baffled, I watched her walk away. Rejection did not happen much in my life, especially not from girls. But this was fine — Meredith was worth it. I could learn to dance.

I mean, how hard could it be?

3

ZOE

$\mathcal{M}$y inflatable unicorn rose and fell with the waves of the Pacific. Sparkles — named for his freckles which shimmered in the sunlight — had a long, golden horn, and two rainbow-colored wings. His eyes were blue, and he had a smile on his face that made him look a bit dumb, but I loved him anyway. When he was fully inflated, there was room for two: me and Nina.

I sprawled across Sparkles, dipping my toes in the water to keep my feet cool. Beside me, Nina adjusted her bathing suit, then squirted another handful of sunscreen on her darkly tanned stomach and rubbed it in. It smelled like coconut and summer.

This was the best part of summer vacation, as far as I was concerned. Floating on the waves, getting a tan — or a burn, in my case — and hanging out with your best friend. We were living our best lives. Aside from my whole "not being able to talk to the boy I liked" problem.

As we bobbed, I eyed the beach.

Highline Hideaway was tucked away from everything.

The nearest parking lot was over a mile away, so if you wanted to visit, you had to park at the main lot for Highline Beach and carry your stuff along a hiking trail that wound through a forest of trees. The path wasn't smooth, either. Gnarled roots crawled across, and tripping and twisting an ankle was a common occurrence.

But Hideaway itself was so beautiful that it made the tough hike worth it. The little, crescent-shaped private beach was all blue ocean, golden sand, and green palm trees. The smell of onion and sausage roasting over fire pits. When the sun set, most of the campfires were snuffed in favor of one giant bonfire. A local craft soda company supplied the wood and paid extra to keep an off-duty police officer on site. They let us party, but they let nothing get out of control.

Naturally, Hideaway was always busy. Mostly Beachbreak High students. And right now, there was one Beachbreaker in particular I was interested in.

Kevin and his friends were on the far end of the beach, hunched over something I couldn't see.

What was it? A board game? A cooler of drinks? Food? I wasn't sure. But now that I was wearing a bathing suit — which was much more flattering than my ratty dance shirt — and deodorant, it was safe to get closer. It was safe to let Kevin see me. I leaned to the side and dipped my hand in the ocean. "Nina. Paddle with me."

Nina groaned. "Can't we just float?"

"No."

"Why not?"

I thought for a moment. "Because we need the exercise?"

"Well now you're just lying. Where do you want to go, even?"

"To the south side."

"But our stuff's on the north side."

"We can go back and get it after." Now I was whining.

Nina took off her sunglasses and looked at me "After what?"

"After I see something."

"See what?" Nina sat up and scanned the south side of the beach. She rolled her eyes so hard the rest of her head moved with them. "Oh. You want to see Mr. Boring."

My lips twitched. Kevin was not boring. He was smart. Polished. "Just because you don't understand what he says, doesn't mean he's boring. It means he's an intellectual."

Nina laughed. "He's not boring because he's smart, he's boring because he's boring. Did you know—"

"No," I said quickly. "We're not playing—"

"Did you know," Nina repeated, grinning, "that Kevin's favorite food is white rice because he thinks brown rice has too much flavor?"

I bit the inside of my cheek to keep from laughing.

Not getting the reaction she hoped for, Nina continued. "Did you know that Kevin's favorite part of the movie is the end credits?"

"You're not funny," I sang, looking away so she couldn't see the traitorous smile on my face.

"Did you know that Kevin's favorite childhood pastime was doing his taxes?"

I snorted and splashed Nina.

She shrieked. "Watch the hair!"

Nina's head of bouncing black curls was her crowning glory. A crowning glory she did not like to get wet.

I grinned. "We're going over there."

Nina cleaned the droplets of water off her sunglasses. "All right. I'll paddle with you, if for no other reason than to make it less obvious that you're spying on him."

"I'm not spying on him," I said. "I'm pining. From a distance. I'm like Romeo with Rosaline."

"Because that's who you want to be compared to: an idiot

who fell in lust with a girl, tore his family apart, then offed himself over a different girl a few days later," Nina said. She shook her head. "Strong romantic role model, that one."

"You're so dramatic."

MASON

*T*he sand burned my feet. I sprinted, skipped, and hopped across the beach, trying to keep my feet in the air as much as possible. When I reached the surf, I dove in headfirst.

Warm ocean water surrounded me.

It was sweet, sweet, relief. There was nothing better than diving into the water on a summer day. I came up for air and floated on my back, fiddling with my plastic sunglasses. They were cheap; I picked them up at Beachbreak's annual music festival for five bucks. Now they were my beach glasses — you never wanted to bring anything expensive to the beach because you were guaranteed to lose it.

Tyler popped out of the water beside me. If I was Mr. All-American, he was the ultimate surf bum. His hair was long now, curling around the nape of his neck, and completely out of control. The boys and I teased him about it. But the girls? They LOVED it.

"There's nothing better than this, my man," I said, floating on my back.

Tyler was standing, scanning the beach.

"Any sign of Parker?" Parker Vanderpost was Tyler's current obsession.

He grinned. "No, but I got something."

"What's that?"

He pointed to an inflatable unicorn that was floating towards the south side of the beach. There were two girls lying on it, and it only took one guess to know who they were. Tyler's little sister, Zoe, and her friend Nina.

Now it was my turn to grin. "Looks like a unicorn got separated from the herd."

"Dangerous for that to happen," Ty said.

I felt for the ground with my feet, then ducked so the water was just at my chin. "Let's have ourselves a unicorn hunt."

ZOE

I crouched on Sparkles. I was trying to be casual, trying to make it look like I was sunning my back. But truthfully, all I was doing was trying to position myself so I could see Kevin — and see what he and his friends were doing.

Kevin stood, the other boys circled around him like students looking up at their teacher. He had one hand behind his back and was gesturing with the other. Explaining something, or maybe giving a lecture. The boys he was talking to looked bored. They probably just didn't understand what he was saying.

Kevin was too smart for a lot of people. In my darkest nightmares, he was also too smart for me. I imagined going on a date with him — in this fantasy, I could actually talk to him — and listening to him as he explained topics that went way over my head. I hoped that didn't happen. It definitely wouldn't happen if I never talked to him, but I did plan to talk to him.

Eventually.

Some day.

When I figured out the perfect thing to say.

"ZOE." Nina's voice made me jump.

"What?"

"I asked you a question."

I shifted uncomfortably, the unicorn squeaking beneath me. "Which was?"

"How did you not hear me? You literally nodded when I asked if you were listening."

I did?

Nina rested her head on her arms. "Out of everyone I've ever met — and I mean everyone — you have the worst one-track mind. If there was a cloud that looked like a cute boy, you would walk off a cliff while trying to follow it."

"I would not."

"You absolutely would. Otherwise, you would remember what I just said." Nina yawned. "But it's fine. I can be the second most important person in your life. Behind whoever your crush of the day is."

"Pfft. Like some boy could ever replace you." The unicorn squeaked again as I adjusted my position to get a better look at Kevin.

"Seriously, when you have a crush, it's all you can think about."

"You're exaggerating." I dipped my arm in the water and paddled, spinning our unicorn slightly so we — I —could get a better view. "I do not have a one-track mind. In fact, I'll have you know that I have a perfect awareness of everything going on at all times. As a dancer, you need to be aware of your surroundings— wait what was—"

Sparkles wobbled. Then, while I was mid-sentence, Sparkles lifted onto his side as if he'd been caught in a hurricane-force gale. Or as if someone had snuck up on us.

We shrieked.
Nina rolled into me.
And then we both fell into the water.

MASON

*T*he unicorn floated on its side, bobbing with the waves, its horn submerged. Tyler stood behind it, laughing.

It had taken us ten minutes to get to the unicorn. Whenever the girls glanced in our direction, we both dove beneath the water, holding our breath for as long as we could. When we got closer, it sounded like they were arguing over something. Whatever it was, it was the perfect distraction.

Zoe emerged from the water, her soaking wet hair covering her face. She pulled her hair out of her eyes and glared. Water spouted from her mouth, and her glare hardened. "I suppose you thought that was hilarious?"

I grinned. There was nothing I enjoyed more than annoying Ty's little sister. Besides football, it might have been my favorite thing to do. Plus, I liked the way she looked when she was angry. Her eyes narrow, her lips pouty. A sleek jungle cat ready to pounce. "I was just trying to help you out," I said. "You two looked like you needed to cool off."

"You're looking pretty hot yourself," she snapped.

I tilted my head. "You think I'm hot and you're only

telling me now? You've had years to confess your feelings, in fact—"

Zoe cut me off with a noise that sounded vaguely like a growl. Then she smiled maliciously. "I think you need to cool down."

Still grinning, I took a step towards her. "You think you're strong enough to dunk me? I'd like to see you try."

"Who said anything about dunking?" Zoe raised her fist. Inside her clamped palm, there was a giant ball of slimy green seaweed. It looked like a tangle of sludge.

"You wouldn't."

"Oh, I would." She hurled the ball of seaweed at me.

ZOE

*M*y beautiful ball of slime arched through the air, its green tendrils flying behind it. When we were younger, and Mason wasn't around, Tyler made me throw the football with him. I liked to believe all those years of training prepared me for this precise moment, when a ball of slime would wipe the smirk off Mason's perfect face.

Mason dove out of the way.

My ball of slime missed.

I shook my head and charged to where Mason dived. There was no way — NO WAY — I was letting him get away with dunking me. Or him saying I thought he was hot. Mason had been best friends with my brother for years now, and I'd watched them grow up together, play football together, and talk about girls incessantly as they got older. They both seemed to have a lot of girls interested in them, goodness knows why. Maybe nobody else could see through Mason's tall, muscular frame, blue-green eyes and tousled blonde hair. But I could.

Mason was like a very large child. And therefore, my relationship with him operated strictly on playground rules. If he did something I didn't like, I didn't go crying to the teacher. I returned the favor. If he put toothpaste in my Oreos, I put vinegar in his water bottle. If I made a sarcastic jab at his expense, he exposed me with a witty comeback. And if he dunked me, I turned him into a seaweed princess.

Something brushed my leg.

Mason.

I squealed, then stomped wildly at the figure lurking beneath the waves. If I was lucky, I'd get a couple good shots in—

His firm hand clamped around my leg. He yanked, hard, and despite years of dance, I didn't have the balance to stay on my feet.

I fell into the water.

But just before I went under, he rose beneath me, positioning my body over his shoulders and lifting me up like I weighed nothing. I supposed to someone as ripped as he was, I probably did weigh almost nothing.

I tried to scramble free. "Don't you dare do it, Mason."

"Do what?" He tightened his grip on my legs.

All I could do was punch helplessly at the muscles in his back. Not that it did anything — his muscles were harder than my fists. I briefly considered pinching him, but that felt like too much of a bratty little sister move. "I swear, if you—"

"Zoe?" Nina sounded as helpless as I felt. It was easy to see why — my brother had her over his shoulder. He was smiling. She was not.

"Aren't we too old for this?" I asked.

Mason ignored me. "On three?"

"One," Tyler said.

I tried to slip free of Mason's grasp. No luck.

"Two…"

Mason quickly repositioned his hands so he was holding my hips.

I held my breath.

"Three!" Mason effortlessly tossed me into the air. He was so strong, that, for a heartbeat, it felt like I was flying. Like I could spread my arms, flap, and I would take off into the sky.

Then gravity kicked in.

Nina and I crashed into the ocean simultaneously.

I kicked hard to get away from Mason. If my brother and him were super bored, they could spend hours tormenting Nina and I, tossing us in the air and teasing us. We needed to counterattack quickly, and for that, I needed space. So, my breath held, I swam underwater, trying to get as far from Mason as possible. I felt for globs of seaweed, but there was none. Fine. No seaweed? Mud was just as effective.

I dug my hand into the goop, enjoying its weight. How much more would I enjoy it when the mud was pressed into Mason's face?

I popped out of the water, my arm curled back, ready to throw. "You're dead—"

Mason and Tyler weren't there anymore.

And neither was Sparkles.

Because, after throwing us, the pair had commandeered Sparkles and were now laying on top of him, swimming as quickly as they could towards the north shore. We would never, ever catch them.

I looked to the sky. Why, oh why, did I have to have an idiot older brother with a maddening best friend? And why couldn't I ever get the upper hand on Mason? Just one time? Was that too much to ask? I let the mud dissolve in my hand.

Nina swam up beside me. "I hate your brother," she said flatly.

"Join the club."

"They took Sparkles."

"They did."

"We can't let that go."

I shook my head. "Oh, we won't."

8

MASON

I sprawled on the inflatable unicorn, letting the sun dry my body. It only took us a few minutes to make it all the way to the north shore. I suspected it would take Zoe and Nina much longer, which gave us time to drag the unicorn onto the sand and relax on the beach. By the time they emerged from the water, the unicorn and I were dry.

"Incoming," Tyler said.

I stretched, trying to look as lazy and relaxed as possible, then took off my sunglasses. I was kind of glad Meredith wasn't at Hideaway today. She probably would've found our hilarious antics childish.

Zoe and Nina stomped across the beach. They looked so angry that if there had been a sand castle in their way, they would've kicked it over just to have something to destroy. A ball of seaweed dripped from Zoe's hand. You had to give her credit — she was not afraid to get dirty.

"You think we went too far?" I asked.

"No way, dude," Tyler said. "Operation bribe?"

"Operation bribe." I hopped off the unicorn, stretched

again, then grabbed the small blue cooler we'd hidden. I cuddled it against my chest.

"Any last words?" Zoe's voice carried across the beach. "You can't save yourself this time, Space Face."

I snickered. At Zoe's eighth birthday party, I accidentally — and it was an accident — made a joke at her expense. Flustered, she replied by calling me "Space Face." We think she meant to call me a "Space Case," but either way, the name stuck. I grinned. "You wouldn't want to throw that ball of seaweed if you knew what was inside this little treasure chest."

Zoe hesitated.

I flipped open the cooler lid, revealing four plastic bowls of ice cream.

Zoe's eyes widened. Her forearm tensed as she gripped the seaweed tighter.

She wasn't still thinking of throwing it, was she? I set the cooler down, then grabbed the cup of ice cream I'd ordered her. I dramatically fell to one knee and presented the bowl to her with both hands, like I was making an offering to an ancient temple. "Triple chip, double fudge, with peanut butter drizzled on top."

Zoe's grip loosened slightly. "So, this is how it is? You think you can dunk me, then make it up with ice cream?"

I poked my head out from behind the bowl and grinned. "Did it work?"

She raised the seaweed.

No. No way—

Then she dropped it and snatched the bowl of ice cream from my hands. "You're lucky, Space Face."

I passed Nina and Tyler their bowls of ice cream, then grabbed my own. "Nah, Zoo," I said. "I'm just that good."

9

ZOE

I spent most Saturdays alone, so it was a pleasant change to be eating ice cream on the beach with other people — even if two of those people happened to be Ty and Mason.

For once, the guys didn't seem interested in chatting up the popular girls from school, and we spent the day lounging in the sand. When it got too hot, we went for a swim or stood in the surf and tossed a frisbee. Then, we brought out Sparkles and took turns racing to the buoy and back. Mason won — although Ty complained bitterly that he cheated. I was surprised at how nice it was to spend time with my brother today. But, as much as I enjoyed my time with everyone, by the time the evening came, I was back to my usual Saturday agenda for introverts: hanging out on the couch by myself.

Tyler's cologne entered the living room before he did. He was wearing khaki shorts and a black t-shirt, and he juggled his keys as he strutted towards the front door. He slipped on his flip-flops, then looked at me. "Got a hot date with Parker tonight," he said. "Don't wait up."

28

"Remember your curfew, Tyler!" Mom yelled from her office.

"Don't worry!" Ty yelled back. He looked at me again, grinned, and shook his head. There was no way he was going to be back by curfew, and we both knew it.

I stifled a laugh.

Ty left.

Without his energy, the house felt quiet. In the distance, I heard the clacking sound of mom's mechanical keyboard. She bought the keyboard after Dad left. She said she liked the noise; it made her feel like there was someone else in the house. I thought that was the saddest thing I'd ever heard, but it made her happy.

Sad or not, lying on the couch with no plans, I understood what she meant. Being alone sucked. Being alone with no noise was worse.

I dug between the cushions until I found the remote, then I searched for a show on Netflix. Somehow, there were a hundred TV shows and a thousand movies, and yet there was nothing I wanted to watch. I settled on a reality show about a baking competition in Australia. It was called "Cakes Don't Rise Down Under," and the host was a chipper Australian who bounced around like he injected caffeine.

"No plans?" Mom stood in the doorway. While Tyler had inherited dad's height and tan complexion, I shared my petite frame, unruly dark hair and pale skin with my mother. "It's Saturday. You should do something."

I winced inwardly. As a general rule, I preferred when people didn't point out my lack of social life. I shrugged. "Everyone's busy."

"You didn't want to go with Tyler?"

"I don't think Ty wants to drag his little sister on a date."

Mom frowned. "He didn't tell me it was a date."

"And that… surprises you?"

"I like to know things." Mom shrugged. "But, if it's just the two of us tonight, how about we do something together?"

I must've been the lamest sixteen-year-old girl in the world. It was the last Saturday night before school started, and the only person who wanted to hang out with me was my mom. I loved my mom, but hanging out with her wasn't quite the same as going on a date with a cute boy. At least, I assumed it wasn't. Still, better Mom than no one. I turned off the TV. "I will do literally anything."

"Cinnamon buns?"

"Done." I followed Mom into the kitchen. If I was being honest, she wasn't a good baker. Mom was forgetful, so when she made cookies, she inevitably forgot to put the chocolate chips in, or left them in the oven an extra five minutes, so the outer edges were burnt black.

Cinnamon buns were an exception to the rule. Why? Because when we made cinnamon buns, we cheated. We didn't make the dough from scratch. Instead, we found out that you could use a tube of pre-made pizza dough and no one would know the difference. It was a thousand times easier.

I grabbed a tube of pizza dough from the fridge, then set the oven to 400F. "Mom, do you think I'm, you know, kind of lame?"

In a small bowl, Mom mixed a tablespoon of cinnamon with three tablespoons of brown sugar. "Of course you're not lame, honey. You're wonderful. Whatever gave you that silly idea?"

Life. I lightly floured the surface of the counter. "You have to say that."

"Even if I wasn't your mom, I wouldn't think you were lame."

I doubted that very much. "Did you date when you were in high school?"

"Ah, so this is what brought all this on." Mom scooped two tablespoons of butter into a dish, shoved it in the microwave, and watched it melt. "I... had a handful of gentlemen callers, if you know what I mean."

I blinked. Did I know what she meant? More importantly, did I want to know? Perhaps, I decided, I should skip this avenue of inquiry. I finished flouring the counter, then I peeled the label off the pizza dough tube and pressed my thumbs to the seam. There was a loud pop, then I pulled out the dough and flattened it.

The microwave beeped. Mom mixed the melted butter with the cinnamon sugar and handed it to me. "Why don't you start by telling me what's on your mind?"

"I don't understand boys," I said simply, smearing the cinnamon mixture onto the dough. "Whenever I talk to one, I feel like I'm doing something wrong."

Mom rubbed my back. "Your feminine urges are nothing to be ashamed—"

"Ew, MOM! That is so, so not what I mean," I said. "And please don't say feminine urges."

Mom looked like she was trying not to laugh. "Sorry, honey. Go on."

"It's just, whenever I talk to someone, or there's a boy I like, I feel like there's this code. Or that there are these rules I don't understand, but everyone else does. What you're supposed to say, how you're supposed to act, what you're supposed to do. Everyone else has these instincts that guide them through. And I don't have those instincts. My instinct is like, to blink at him awkwardly, laugh too loudly, then drool on my shirt. I'm very lady-like."

Mom laughed. She greased a pan. "You want to know what the big secret is?"

Hope fluttered in my stomach. Was there a big secret?

31

Some little thing I could do, or correct? I looked at mom, waiting for the answer to all of my woes.

She set the pan down and hugged me. "You just need to be yourself."

My fragile balloon of hope popped. That was definitely not the answer I was looking for. Somehow, I suspected boys weren't interested in the weird girl that gawked at them from afar, then dove behind park benches when they looked her way. I hugged mom back anyway. "I'll try."

"Good," Mom said. "Now, if it's ok with you, I'm going to go squeeze in another few minutes of work here, if you can finish up?"

Mom worked long, hard, antisocial hours on her real estate business. I knew that everything she did, she did it for Tyler and I. "I'll take it from here."

"Thanks, honey. We can watch a movie after. Your pick. As long as Channing Tatum's in it."

"Deal." I rolled the dough, then cut it into small cinnamon buns, then arranged them on the pan and shoved them in the oven. My mom was great at two things: loving me unconditionally and giving me platitudes. She saw me in the best possible light. To her, all of my many, many flaws, were just adorable little quirks. They were what made me, me.

I set a timer on my cell phone, then went back to watching Cakes Don't Rise Down Under. The host poked a brownie with a toothpick and the toothpick came out covered in chocolate goop. Unbaked. Which was how I felt. I needed more time to figure things out, I needed someone to help me. Someone who knew how to date.

A girl like that wouldn't be easy to find in my small circle. Nina was eternally single. Kenzie had been in one relationship that failed spectacularly. Callie spent a lot of time surfing with her very cute neighbor Jace, but whenever we pressed her about him, she claimed she wasn't interested.

And there weren't any other girls I was close enough to ask for advice from.

Though, now that I thought about it, why did I need the advice to come from a girl? Tyler was currently on a date. Maybe he could help me.

Ha. No. Ty was my big brother, and as much as he teased me, he would have the same problem Mom did: he wouldn't ever acknowledge my real flaws.

I needed someone who I trusted enough not to hurt me with their criticism, but who was willing to be honest about whatever it was that I was doing wrong.

An idea hit me and I practically leaped from the couch.

I knew who I needed.

I needed the boy that would dunk me in the ocean, but then buy me ice cream after.

10

MASON

*T*he sights and sounds of pre-season football filled the kitchen. Helmets and pads crashed together, announcers diagramed plays, and the crowd booed whenever the refs threw a flag.

I stood at the kitchen island, my eyes fixed on my laptop, which was streaming a game between the 49ers and the Broncos. My dad hated preseason football. Pointless, he called it. The starters only played for a quarter, so you were stuck watching backups the rest of the game.

That's what I liked. Players, only a few years older than me, thrown into the lion's den. There were mistakes, miscommunications. How did you adjust when the player beside you missed their assignment? Football was the ultimate team sport. If you didn't work together, you lost. And there was something cool about learning to work together with someone you barely knew.

The game cut to a commercial.

I found a bottle of Ranch dressing in the refrigerator door, uncapped it, and sprayed it liberally over two chicken and bacon wraps. I tucked my laptop under my arm, then

34

carried two plates upstairs and kicked my sister's bedroom door. She didn't answer immediately, so I kicked it again.

I could practically hear her rolling her eyes.

The door swung open.

"Oh-em-gee, what?" Chelsey looked at me like I was the single biggest imposition on her life. Then she saw the wraps and her eyes went wide.

"Is this a bribe? So early in the year? What did you do this time? Tell me EVERYTHING."

"Nothing," I said, handing her the wrap. Chelsey was always suspicious of me. And, to be fair, with the amount of times I'd broken curfew — or the other rules I didn't see the point in — she was right to be suspicious. "Think of it as a preemptive bribe. Just in case."

Chelsey took the chicken wrap. "Extra Ranch?"

"Obviously."

"Hmmm." She examined the wrap suspiciously. "You never make me food unless you've done something wrong. You must be expecting a lot of trouble. Did you get kicked off the team or something?"

I laughed. "They'd never kick me off the team. I just want you to stay out of my way for the afternoon. And don't come to my room."

"Okay, weirdo." Chelsey took a bite of her wrap, closed her eyes, and smiled. "Mmm… Ranch. Toodles."

She kicked the door shut.

Chelsey was two years younger than me and even more strong-willed. As a result, we used to butt heads constantly. If I said the sky was blue, she'd insist it was actually royal blue, which was a completely different kind of blue, so I was obviously wrong. However, although we made natural enemies, there was one thing that united us: Dad.

As a single parent, he wasn't strict, but he was horribly inconsistent. Monday, you take the car out for a spin and back into a light post and he laughs it off. Tuesday, you get a C+ on a test and he grounds you for two weeks. It was easier for Chelsey and me to police ourselves using a complicated system of bribes.

But that's not why I was bribing her today.

I was bribing her today because if she came into my room and saw what was happening, it would've destroyed my reputation.

My bedroom was at the end of the hall. Everything inside was one size too small for me. It was a downside to being 6'2". When I laid on my bed, I couldn't straighten out or my feet would hang off the end. Part of the ceiling was on an angle, so I had to duck if I wanted to use that side of my room. And glue and duct tape held together my desk and chair.

I flipped open my laptop and made my first search: How to Two-Step. I clicked on the first video that appeared. It was an older woman wearing blue jeans, a blouse with a stitched flower, and a white cowboy hat. She tipped her hat as the video started, then explained how to two-step.

I devoured my wrap as I watched, trying to mirror the footwork with what I was seeing on screen. Meredith had better appreciate all of this effort.

Left, right, quick step. Left, right, quick step. Easy enough.

The woman introduced her partner. He was practically made of denim. The woman tipped her hat to the camera. "Y'all, I can't stress enough how important it is for y'all to have a partner when you're learning. You need to learn to feel your partner and read their body, and every partner's different."

Maybe the average person needed a partner, but I didn't. I didn't want one, either. Imagine if word got out that the starting quarterback was trolling Beachbreak looking for dance partners. I couldn't let that happen — I had a reputation to protect. And I wasn't interested in dealing with the boys taking shots at me every time I stepped on the field. They'd probably call me "Twinkle Toes" or something stupid.

I mirrored the dance steps in time with the music. Left, right, quick-step. Left, right, quick-step.

"This next one's a bit of a trick," the woman said. She danced with the man, he lifted his hand, she spun, then when he pulled her back, he lifted his hand and she spun the other way.

I circled my room, practicing the move. But without a partner, I was just an idiot raising my hand in the air. Maybe the video lady was right. Maybe I did need a partner.

I sat at my desk and looked up dance classes. There were a handful, but all of them were in the evenings when I had football practice.

Well, I would just have to beat the odds and learn to dance without a partner.

Rejection was not an option.

ZOE

*B*y every account, Beachbreak High was beautiful. Most of the campus was outdoors, with lockers lining the brick pathways that connected the classrooms. The cafeteria was also outside, with stone benches and tables resting beneath a pergola. And, best of all, it was close to the ocean. So close, in fact, that no matter where you were on campus, you could hear the crash of the tide, the squawk of seagulls, and occasionally the honk of a large ship.

Near shore, there was a grassy knoll where people liked to hang out between classes. Currently, the knoll was occupied by Kevin, who was engaged in a game of chess with one of his friends.

I curled my fingers around the strap on my backpack, and I watched from afar. I'd carefully put together my "First Day of School" outfit, selecting a jean skirt and white top I hoped would simultaneously make me blend in and look cute. I'd flat ironed my hair. Worn lip gloss. I'd even prepared a few things to say. But at the sight of Kevin, blood rushed to my ears, my mouth went dry, and talking became impossible.

So instead, I stared.

From a distance.

Like a normal person.

Ugh, get it together, Zoe.

"If you want him to notice you, you're going to have to talk to him." The voice belonged to Nina, who had snuck up behind me while I was lost in my daydreams.

"You don't know that," I said. "Maybe he'll notice me from a distance. Or maybe we'll have some classes together this semester. Then I can sit beside him. And eventually, he'll ask me for a pencil. Or I'll ask him for a pencil. Whichever."

"Or you could not wait for fate and just talk to him?"

I snorted. "Like that would ever work. Remember the last boy I liked and tried to talk to?"

"Chris Stewart?" Nina frowned. "What happened to him?"

"He said meeting me was so awkward that he convinced his family to move to Florida." Okay. That was a slight exaggeration. But the one conversation we ever had involved me stumbling into him, not knowing where to look, and somehow directly addressing the pimple on his nose for the entire chat — cut short by Chris putting a hand over his face and leaving. For good. It was probably the least graceful moment of my existence — and that's a high bar.

The bell rang.

Nina grabbed my elbow. "Come on. Let's start our junior year with a bang."

MASON

I waited for the bell to stop ringing. I was supposed to be in chemistry, snagging one of two science classes I still needed to graduate. Instead, I was standing in the administrator's office, holding a tablet, and swiping through class options. There was one dance class that still had openings this semester. Introduction to Dance. Unlike the advanced classes, it didn't require an audition or a teacher's recommendation, only enthusiasm.

"What do you think?" I asked, eyeing the tablet.

"I think you're taking this too seriously, dude." Tyler stood behind me, casually holding his backpack so it was dragging on the ground.

"Meredith won't go to Homecoming with me unless I learn to dance," I said. "And a girl like that — she's got options. College boys. College boys that can dance. You remember her ex?"

Ty thought for a moment, then shrugged and shook his head. "Dude, just go to Homecoming with someone else. Lots of girls would be stoked to snag an invite."

"It's not about that," I said. I knew Tyler was right — if I wanted to, I'd have no trouble finding a date for Homecoming. But I didn't want just any date. I wanted the right date. I wanted one that was a challenge. I wanted one that didn't think I'd ever be able to dance. Someone I could prove wrong. And when I proved her wrong, she would see a whole new side of me. And be my date.

I gave Tyler the side eye. "You don't think I can do it, do you? You don't think I can dance."

Ty yawned and leaned against the wall; his arms crossed. Somehow every move he made was so casual, so relaxed. No wonder he could get a date with Parker Vanderpost. He was probably the only guy in school not impressed with her status. "Dance if you want. But when the boys find out—"

"I know, I know." If you were on the football team, and anyone found out you did something classified as "girly," you'd get roasted. If they found out I was interested in dance, they'd call me "Twinkle Toes," hide a tutu in my locker, and play ballet music during pep rallies. I was a confident guy, but I wasn't about to hang myself up like a pinata.

I checked the dance class schedule again. If I wanted to take Introduction to Dance, I'd have to push back Life Skills — another course I needed to graduate. And if I moved Life Skills to next semester, I'd end up missing the math credit I needed.

"It doesn't matter," I said. "There's no way I can make my schedule work."

"Here." Tyler took the tablet from me and swiped through the options. Ty was laid back — some would say lazy — but, like his sister, he was smart. Top of his class when he tried — which was almost never. If anyone ever figured out how to unlock his potential, they'd have a gem on their hands. He shrugged and handed the tablet back. "Who cares about the class? You don't need the class to learn to dance."

We exited the admin building. The cafeteria, which sat at

the center of Beachbreak, was empty. That made sense — no one wanted to be late on the first day. I was lucky. As the starting quarterback, no one cared if I was late on the first day. Teachers were usually thrilled when I showed up, for some reason. I headed towards the chemistry labs. "How else am I going to learn? I tried online videos, man. It's a bust."

"You don't need a class, dude, you need a teacher."

"Meredith won't teach me."

Tyler opened the door to class. "Good thing I'm not talking about Meredith."

ZOE

*B*y lunch time, I was exhausted. It felt like I'd left my brain off all summer, and now, like a dusty computer with whirring fans and flashing lights, it was desperately trying to turn on and stay awake. My morning started with biology, then dance. I liked to schedule dance right before lunch, because our dance teacher would let us go ten minutes early so we could shower.

Nina, Kenzie, and Callie were waiting for me in the cafeteria.

I waved to them, loaded up a tray with a pizza bagel and a blue slushie, and sat down. Nina was wearing one of her trademark band shirts. I hadn't seen this one before. It featured a delivery truck backing a piano into a moving space. An old man stood on the sidewalk, shouting for the truck to "Keep Baching Up."

"Funny." I nodded at her shirt and took a bite of my bagel. The molten hot cheese scorched my tongue.

"Your morning?" Kenzie asked, looking up from her textbook.

I pretended to fall asleep.

"You and me both, sister," Callie said. "Want to skip out and catch some waves?"

Kenzie glared. "You shouldn't skip class. And you definitely shouldn't skip on the first day. It sets a bad precedent."

Callie shrugged. "I like to keep the bar low. That way I get bonus points just for showing up."

Kenzie made a disgusted noise and Callie grinned. Somehow, they were simultaneously best friends and worst enemies. Kenzie was on track for Harvard and involved in extracurricular clubs I didn't even know existed. Callie spent ninety percent of her waking time in the water, and it was not unusual for her to show up three hours late to events, her clothes damp and sand in her hair.

All too soon, the bell rang. I hoped that the pizza bagel and slushie would give me enough energy to get through the rest of my day, but as I dragged myself to Life Skills, I could already feel the tendrils of a sugar coma about to drag me to the depths of sleep.

But, when I arrived at Life Skills, who should I see sitting in the back corner of the class, playing on his phone? Mason. His t-shirt was the perfect size, highlighting his broad shoulders, and just tight enough so it hugged his biceps. The surrounding seats were empty, but a pair of junior girls sat on the other side of the classroom and stared at him. If I looked in their eyes, I suspected their pupils would be shaped like little hearts.

I ignored the urge to give them a roll of paper towel to wipe the drool off their desks and instead went and sat beside Mason. For once, he was just the person I wanted to see.

"Fancy seeing you here."

Mason smiled and pocketed his phone. "Hey, Zoo. Nice to see someone I actually know."

"You know everybody." I pointed out.

"Other way around," Mason said. "Everyone knows me. Me? I know nobody."

Typical freaking Mason.

"Okay, Mr. Popular." I made a face at him.

He laughed. "It's not all it's cracked up to be. Believe me."

I doubted that. Life would be so easy if people bent over backwards to serve me everywhere I went. Imagine walking into a classroom, twenty minutes late, and having the teachers thank you for showing up? That was Mason's life. Or, more accurately, the life of any star quarterback in a school that cared about football. "Why are you doing Life Skills in your senior year?"

"Kept pushing it off," Mason said. "Didn't have time."

"Too busy dating every girl in your class?" I flinched as the words came out of my mouth. My plan, such as it was, was to circle our conversation to dating, then segue into asking him to teach me what he knows. In my head, the conversation was a lot less clumsy. But that was basically my life — smooth in my head, embarrassingly awkward in real life. I looked away from Mason, trying to play it cool.

"Didn't think you were that interested in my dating life, Zoo."

I didn't have a response.

Fortunately, I didn't need one. Our Life Skills teacher, Mrs. Cortez, waltzed in. She wore a white blouse and black slacks, and skipped straight over new semester greetings of any sort. "Life Skills. Most students treat this as a blow-off class. Something they have to pass so they can get their diploma. But, realistically, this is the most important class many of you will take. Ever."

That seemed unlikely.

"You will work in pairs on a semester-long life development project. During that project, you and your partner will each build a fake life. You will find jobs, living accommodations. You will get married — or not — you will budget for vacations, and you will deal with whatever disasters I throw your way. Because if there is one thing you should know about your life, it's that it will never go exactly how you plan it."

"Depressing," I muttered.

Mason smirked. "Where's your sense of adventure?"

"Forgot it at home."

He snorted.

Mrs. Cortez circled the classroom and handed out our first assignment. It was a single sheet of paper with multiple choice options that showed what our lives could look like. We could get married and have kids, get married and not have kids, or stay single. There was also a long list of career options, everything from the practicality of an accountant, to the fantasy of a traveling concert musician. There was also a list of different cities we could live in.

Mason nudged me. "Want to partner up?"

"Sure." I scanned the assignment. How realistic were we supposed to be filling in our answers? "Since I have had zero luck in the dating department, I should probably just select single and lives with her cat."

Mason snickered. "I'm thinking of being a rodeo clown."

"Well, you know how to be a clown, so the rodeo probably isn't much of a stretch." I grinned.

"Do you think they make the big bucks?"

"Not as much as a neurosurgeon."

"You're going to be a neurosurgeon?"

"Only if it means I can operate myself and fix the part of my brain that's supposed to understand boys," I said.

Mason skimmed his paper. "What don't you know about boys?"

"It's not just boys," I said. "It's dating. And it's everything. Like whenever there's anything dating related, or I even try to talk to a boy I like, it's a disaster. It's like there's all these rules that everyone else is following, but no one told me what they are."

Mason looked at me suspiciously, but said nothing.

I felt nervous, but I didn't know why. I'd known Mason my entire life. And, while he loved to tease me and prank me, he wasn't the type to make fun of me about something that actually mattered — like not knowing how to get a date.

But I also couldn't tell if he was picking up on the hints I was laying down. Maybe you had to be blunt with boys. "You're pretty good at dating."

Mason grinned. "Some would say I'm the best."

I rolled my eyes. "Only because you're hot."

"Excellent use of flattery," Mason said.

"Thanks," I replied. "Flattery's what us average people use so we can compete."

"Oh please, Zoo. As if you're average."

I went cold and narrowed my eyes. Maybe this wasn't such a good idea. "What?"

"You're way better than average."

Heat rose to my cheeks, and I had to look away quickly. Mason was just being nice. Just being a good friend. He didn't mean anything by it — so I shouldn't read into it. At all. "Well, being not-average hasn't helped me get any dates. So clearly there's something wrong."

"It's like you said — you don't know the rules."

So there WERE rules.

Mason stretched and put his hands behind his head. "Lucky for you, you're sitting next to someone who knows the rules. And this is Life Skills — and dating is definitely a life skill you'll want to know."

Well, this was going better than expected. Time to put my cards on the table. "Will you teach me?"

47

Mason leaned close, keeping his voice low. "I'll help you out. But if I help you, you need to help me."

"What could I possibly help you with?"

Mason checked around to make sure no one was looking. "Dance."

"You want me to—"

Mason clamped his hand over my mouth. "Quiet, Zoo. Man."

I had the urge to lick his hand, just to gross him out a little. But that probably would've jeopardized any chance of getting him to teach me how to date. Even longtime friends could only stand so much grossness.

He removed his hand. "I asked Meredith to Homecoming."

Meredith Byrd. Tall. Blonde. Beautiful. And easily the best dancer on the dance team. I was in awe of her skill, her poise.

"Bold," I said. "I heard she was dating a guy from USC."

Mason's mouth twitched. "She's not. But she'll only go to Homecoming with someone who knows how to dance."

That made sense. Every Homecoming, Beachbreak High had a giant dance competition for any couple that wanted to participate. A couple from the dance team almost always won. And since Meredith was the captain, she probably saw it as her right to win. But she needed the right partner. "So," I said, crossing my arms, "the mighty Space Face comes to me for help."

"You came to me first," Mason pointed out. "But yes, I need your help too. You're the best dancer I know."

"You mean the best dancer you know that will put up with you."

"That's right." Mason grinned. "So, what do you say? Do we have a deal?"

It took me a microsecond to shake his hand. "Let's do it."

14

ZOE

*M*y day was almost, almost over. In fact, I only had one class left: Physics, with the notoriously grumpy Mr. Hinshaw.

He paced across the classroom, his gnarled hands twisted behind his back. The buttons on his collared shirt strained against the bulge of his belly. "We will begin this year, as we do every year, with a quiz."

Normally, a pop quiz would make my stomach sink and make my palms sweaty. But by the end of my first day back, I was too tired to care. I took the quiz, scribbling my answers, trying to remember any formula at all. When I was finished, I brought my paper to the front of the class and stood beside Mr. Hinshaw's desk while he marked it.

Blue checkmark.

Red X.

Red X.

Red X.

Red X.

Blue checkmark.

Red X.

By the time he was finished scrawling X's on my paper, his pen was running out of ink. Scowling, he handed my paper back, then took Nina's, uncapped a second pen, and repeated the process. When everyone had handed in their tests, Mr. Hinshaw had gone through three red pens.

His wrinkled jowls quivered. "This quiz covered everything you will learn in my Physics class. None of you passed. If you follow my logic, this means that there is not a single student in this class who already knows the subject matter we will discuss. As such, it behooves you to be quiet when I speak."

"I think it behooves me to switch out of this class," Nina whispered.

I nodded, examining all the red X's on my quiz. This was going to be a long semester of Physics. A very, very long semester. And the worst part? It was the hardest class on my schedule, and it was at the end of the day, when I was tired and wanted to go home. "Bad move," I said. "Putting our hardest class in fourth period."

My normally positive, upbeat friend was slumped in her seat, staring vacantly at the chalkboard. "If we work together, we can get through this. I have to believe that."

"It's our only option," I agreed. "And speaking of working together, I found someone who will teach me how to date."

Nina raised an eyebrow. "Is Kenzie finally ready to talk?"

"Not her," I said. Kenzie was the only girl in our friend group who'd been in a real relationship. It ended in disaster, and she never, ever talked about it. No matter how much prying we did. "Mason wants to help."

Nina's jaw dropped. "Mason?"

I nodded excitedly.

She pressed her lips together, frowning. "Hmm."

"What?"

Nina shifted in her chair. She waited until Mr. Hinshaw

was pacing towards the other end of the classroom, then continued. "Are you sure he's the best person to go to for advice?"

My excitement faded slightly. Twenty minutes ago, I'd been so sure of my plan. But now, Nina was trying to poke holes in it — which usually meant she noticed something I didn't. Something that would be a problem. "Why not Mason? If anyone knows the rules of dating, it's him."

"Come on, Zoe," Nina said. "Rules don't apply to guys like Mason. He's the starting quarterback. He's gorgeous. Half the school is already in love with him. He could walk up to any single girl in school, burp, then ask them out, and they'd still say yes."

"First — gross," I said. "And second, just because the rules don't apply to Mason doesn't mean he doesn't know what the rules are. He's been on so many dates, he's probably lost count. He has experience — and experience is what I lack. Besides, it's not like there's a better option. Kenzie won't talk, and Ty's not exactly unbiased."

"Fine. Maybe there's not a better option. But..." Nina cut herself off.

It wasn't like her to hold back. "Out with it."

"I don't get why he's helping you."

"Out of the goodness of his heart."

Nina rolled her eyes. "Sure, but why's he actually helping you."

I lowered my voice further. "You can't tell anyone."

"Promise."

"We made a deal," I said. "He teaches me to date, and..."

"And?"

I sighed. "And I teach him how to dance."

"Dance? Why would he want to dance?"

"Because he wants to take Meredith Byrd to Homecoming. And she will only—"

51

"Go with a guy who dances, yeah." Nina looked puzzled.

Why wouldn't she get on board with my plan? It would benefit our entire group. Sure, Mason would teach me directly, but anything I learned, I could pass onto her. "What now?"

"Nothing."

"You have a look."

"It's not any of my business."

"When has that stopped you before?"

Nina glared, then nodded. "Fine. For this to work, you're going to have to spend a lot of time close to each other. Like a lot of time. It's not like dancing, or dating, are easy to learn."

"So?"

She shifted in her seat.

I'd never seen her look so uncomfortable.

She took a deep breath. "Aren't you worried that spending that much time with a really hot guy can lead to... you know... feelings?"

What?

Feelings?

I blinked, then wild laughter burst from my chest.

Mr. Hinshaw sneered. "Physics is serious business, Miss Walsh. And I would advise you not to interrupt me again. And perhaps pay attention."

"Sorry, Mr. Hinshaw." I stopped laughing. Mostly. My shoulders were still shaking slightly, but I thought I was hiding it well enough. When I was sure our grumpy teacher wasn't looking, I turned to Nina. "You cannot be serious."

"Why not?"

"Because it's Mason," I said. "I've spent infinite amounts of time with him."

"Alone?"

"Well, no, but... it's Mason," I repeated. How could I make

this clearer? "He's the boy who used to yank on my pigtails. Who would steal my — our — ice cream. He is definitely not interested in me like that. Trust me. He dates girls like Meredith. Tall, beautiful, confident. I'm short, average, and awkward. I am not on his radar as remotely dateable. He's best friends with my brother. Plus, I'm not interested in him. I'm only getting him to teach me so I can maybe actually say five non-embarrassing words to You Know Who."

Nina sighed. "If you say so."

I fought the urge to laugh again. Me and Mason? That was the most ridiculous thing I'd heard in my life.

15

MASON

*M*y cleats dug into the turf as I took a three-step drop. I pump faked, waited for Tyler to make an outside cut at the pylon, then whipped the ball in his direction. He extended his hands, caught the ball, and instinctively tucked it under his arm.

He jogged back to the start position.

"Nice catch," I said. "Orc, jump in and get your reps."

Oliver "Orc" Peters was the backup quarterback. He was my height, had a jaw like a brick, and a nose that popped out like cauliflower. He jogged past me, grabbed a ball, and started throwing.

It was a hot afternoon, perfect for a swim. Maybe if Coach cut practice early enough, the boys and I could head down to the beach. Ironically, we'd do the same thing we did at practice — bring a ball, stand in the ocean, and throw it back and forth. We wouldn't scrimmage, not this close to the first game of the season. Coach would kill us if someone got injured.

I grabbed a water bottle and tossed a second to Tyler. I sprayed my face, then took a drink. "Gotta thank you, man," I said. "Zoo says she's up for being my dance teacher."

"Don't mention it, dude. Just don't break her feet by stepping all over her." Tyler took a swig. Even with his hair matted from wearing his helmet, he still looked like a tanned beach bum. If you told me he was a professional surfer, I would've believed you. "She charging you for lessons?"

"Not exactly," I said. I finished the water bottle and tossed it on the pile of empties. Our trainers would clean and sterilize them so they were ready for the next practice. "You're going to hear about it anyway, so figure you should hear it from me. Zoo said she'll teach me to dance if I teach her how to date."

Tyler looked away briefly. He splashed more water on his face. "You're telling me that my awkward little sister has suddenly decided she's going to be all grown up?"

"Something like that."

He adjusted his jersey. "Good. She needs something to get her out of the house on Saturday nights. While you're at it, teach her how to relax. Pull a two-fer and teach Nina, too."

I laughed. "I'll start with Zoe. If that goes well, I'll turn this into an entire school. Take over Life Skills class with Mason's Dating for Dummies."

Orc took a five-step drop and whistled the ball to one of the junior receivers. The pass came with heat, but it was off target by a good five yards.

"How're you going to do it?" Ty asked. "Are you going to start your lessons with all the reasons why she should stay away from boys like you?"

I bumped my shoulder pad into his. "What's this, your big brother speech?"

"Totally," Tyler said. He pretended to growl. "You stay away from my sister, you hear? If you don't, blah blah blah, patriarchy, blah."

I chuckled.

Tyler grinned. "Nah, dude. Zoe's smart. Smarter than me when I was her age."

"She's smarter than you now."

"Smarter than both of us."

"Put together."

"Probably," Tyler said. "It's all good, dude. She may be awkward, but she's got a good head on her shoulders. She's not the type to stand for a guy who doesn't treat her well. Not after what she saw with Dad."

The divorce was finalized three years ago, but the scars would last a lifetime. That summer, Tyler stayed at my house almost every night. Zoe was usually with Nina. Neither of them talked about it much, but from what I heard, their Dad did his best to make the divorce as miserable as possible. Word was he was now in Chicago, but no one seemed to know for sure. Zoe and Tyler had never gone out to visit.

"Plus," Tyler said, "my sister's way too smart for a hard-head like you."

He wasn't wrong. I was way, way too much of a classic meathead for Zoe. I did okay in my classes — I was never in danger of failing — but I wasn't anywhere near the honor roll, either. Except in gym, but that barely counted as a real class. And Zoe? She preferred intellectuals. Bookworms. Guys who liked chess, apparently.

Me? I couldn't imagine anything more boring than spending an afternoon staring at a chessboard, contemplating my next move. I wanted to be out in the sun, doing something active. I listened to audiobooks when I was working out, but I wasn't sure Zoe would count that as "reading."

"It's the best of both worlds," I said, putting my helmet back on. "She gets a date with Kevin. I get a date with Meredith."

"Everyone wins," Tyler agreed. "Guess that means I'll have to save my big brother speech for Kevin."

"You should start practicing," I said. "You're the least scary person on the planet."

"Yeah, I'll start practicing if it looks like you can actually get Zoe a date," Ty said. "You got the hard part of the deal. I love my sister to death, but her social awareness is in the negatives. Good luck teaching her."

I jogged back onto the field. "Don't worry about that. I got a plan."

16

ZOE

*O*n Tuesday, Mason started dropping hints about his big plans for teaching me how to date. I actually felt excited. Maybe he was onto something. Maybe I could learn the skills I needed to pick up boys. Somehow, I resisted texting Mason repeatedly asking what his plan was. I was the person who liked to be prepared. Mason was obviously the type of person who liked to make people wait. Watch them sweat a little.

Then, in Life Skills on Friday, Mason finally made his move.

We were looking for a small town we could live in for our fake lives. Mason closed his eyes and pointed to a map, his finger landing on a small town near Denver called Evermore. I'd never heard of it, but it seemed nice.

Mason finished scrolling through photos of the town, then set his phone aside. "So?" He asked. "Are you ready for your first lesson?"

I looked at him, confused. "I thought there was a game tonight?"

"There is. But your lesson's not tonight. It's right now."

I swallowed nervously. Right here, right now? What if someone was listening? I was awkward, sure, but I didn't want the entire school to know that I was so awkward that I didn't have a clue what I was doing with boys. Was there anything more embarrassing than getting dating advice? "What if someone hears us?"

Mason leaned back in his chair, crossed his arms, and shook his head. "For this whole teaching thing to work, you need to be a better student."

I narrowed my eyes. It was probably the first time in my life anyone had accused me of being a poor student. Other than Mr. Hinshaw, but I was sure he just had a grudge. "Maybe if you were a better teacher and told me what you had in mind?"

"Nope," he said. "You just have to trust me."

I bit my lip. I couldn't think of a way around this. "Fine," I said. "But if I have to trust you blindly, then when I teach you to dance, you're going to have to trust me blindly."

He grinned. "I have the utmost faith in you."

"All right. So, what's my first lesson?"

"First, we need to get out of class."

I looked at the clock. We were only 15 minutes into the class. "So, my first lesson is to learn to be more patient?"

He shook his head. "No. Grab your stuff."

"I can't just walk out of class," I said.

"Oh, Zoo, you have a lot to learn." He shoved his binder in his backpack. "Come on."

Um, and how was this going to work? I definitely wasn't the type to just walk out of class whenever I felt like it. I stole a nervous glance at the teacher, then slid my binder into my backpack. I slung it over my shoulder and tentatively followed Mason to the front of the room.

"Mrs. Cortez," Mason said.

Our teacher looked up from the textbook she was reading. "Yes, Mason?"

"You mind if Zoe and I get some fresh air? We want to do some practice interviews — Zoe's going to be a neurosurgeon — but it's a little loud in here."

I wanted to smack him. He could've at least come up with a better excuse. But, to my surprise, our teacher nodded.

"Thanks," Mason said. Then he walked out of the class as if what had just happened was the most natural thing ever.

I ran to catch up with him. "How did you do that?"

He looked at me strangely. "Do what?"

"Get out of class like that. You practically walked out."

He shrugged, his football jersey pulling tight across his chest. "I didn't walk out. I asked the teacher."

I rolled my eyes. "Different rules really do apply to you, don't they?"

He grinned and slung his arm around my shoulder. "Maybe so. But you should be happy — that means they apply to you too, as long as you're with me."

I struggled to hide the smile creeping across my face. This was my first taste of being one of the cool kids, being one of the ones who could get away with anything. What else could I get away with?

I shook my head. No, Zoe. Don't go mad with power. You haven't even passed your first lesson yet.

"So where are we headed?"

"This way," Mason said. He pushed open a door, and we stepped out into the beautiful late August sun. The grass was green, the sky blue, the air warm. It was the perfect summer day. Mason closed his eyes and took a deep breath. "Man, nothing beats being outside."

"What's my first lesson?"

"Eager, aren't you?"

"I've literally been waiting all week for this."

"Won't be much longer now," Mason said. He motioned for me to follow. The cafeteria was mostly empty, except for a couple people studying. We headed towards the beach.

"You're just using this as an excuse to work on your tan, aren't you?"

"Call it multitasking." He slid his sunglasses on. "Okay. The first thing you need to know about men. They're dumb and they don't notice things. Which is why the woman always makes the first move when she's interested."

Well, that didn't seem accurate. Mason must've seen the doubt on my face.

"They do," he insisted. "You're just a lot more subtle about it. You don't need to ask the guy out. You just need to put yourself in his proximity. So he notices you. And so that's what we're going to do today."

We came over the small hill. The beach was beneath us, but just before the beach, there was a flat grassy patch with a pair of stone chessboards. Kevin was sitting at one chessboard by himself, staring down at the plastic pieces. Analyzing something.

My heart jumped to my throat. "I'm not ready for this."

Mason shrugged. "It's exposure therapy."

"I don't want to be exposed."

"Don't worry about that," Mason said. "That's not 'til lesson three."

I smacked his shoulder. "Not. Funny."

Mason smirked. "It was a little funny. Relax, Zoo. All we're going to do is set up at the chessboard beside him and have ourselves a game."

"Great," I said sarcastically. "Too bad I know nothing about chess."

"It won't matter." Mason started towards the chessboards before I could stop him. "Here's another secret about men.

Not one of us can resist playing the hero to a damsel in distress."

"Sexist, much?"

Mason shrugged. "I'm just here to tell you the rules. Can't help if you like them or not."

We sat at the chessboard next to Kevin's. The stone seats were warm from the sun.

Mason unzipped his backpack and pulled out a Ziploc bag with all the pieces.

He arranged them on the board in what I assumed was the correct order. I knew the basics of chess, but I could never remember what positions the pieces were supposed to go in. Was the queen supposed to be on her own color, or was that the king?

I had to give him credit though — Mason was prepared for this lesson. The chess figures in the bag looked cheap, like they were from the dollar store. I was willing to bet he bought them just for today. If nothing else, at least he was taking this seriously.

Kevin didn't pay any attention to us. He would check his phone, then move a piece. Was he re-creating a game? I had heard of people doing that before when they were trying to learn something. Or maybe he was playing someone online. Was that still a thing?

Mason chuckled. "I can't believe you think you can beat me. I'm the best at literally everything I do. And it's such a simple game, it's not complicated like checkers." Mason's ocean eyes glittered. He was up to something here.

Kevin looked at us, looked at Mason, then at the chessboard. The corner of his mouth twitched. Then he returned his focus to his own game.

Mason finished setting up the pieces. "This is going to be the easiest $20 I've ever made," he said. "Okay. My turn. Black always goes first."

"White," Kevin said.

"What?"

"White always goes first," Kevin said. He was right. Even I knew that.

Mason waved the thought away. "It doesn't really matter. It's basically whoever brings the pieces gets to decide."

"That's not how it works," Kevin insisted.

Mason shrugged. "It is today. Besides, I always win when I go first."

"No one always wins," Kevin said.

"I do when I'm playing people like Zoe," Mason said. He was acting the part of a cocky jerk perfectly. But why?

"How much are you playing for?" Kevin asked.

"Twenty big ones," Mason said. "Wanna put some money on me? Could double up."

Kevin licked his lips. "I want to put some money on this. But not on you. How about this? If you're so good, you'll probably have no problem beating me and Zoe put together. I'll even give you two-to-one odds."

Mason pretended to consider this. Then he motioned for me to slide to the side. "All right. Two against one."

Kevin left his game and sat on the stool beside me, our shoulders touching. My palms sweat. He smelled like fresh printer paper. It was probably the closest he'd ever been to me. I always wondered what he smelled like.

Was that a creepy thing to think?

"Game on," Mason said.

Kevin nodded, eyeing the board seriously.

The game, as you would expect, was a massacre. After a handful of opening moves, every move Kevin made was taking one of Mason's pieces. First his castle, and his knight, then his queen. Within ten minutes, Mason's king was surrounded.

"Checkmate," Kevin said.

Mason frowned. Then, he opened his Ziploc bag, and started collecting pieces. "I have to go to practice. He probably just got lucky."

"Don't forget to pay the lady," Kevin said.

Mason glared, pulled out his wallet, and handed me a crisp twenty.

I offered it to Kevin. "I think you did most of the work."

He refused to take it. "We were a team."

I knew he was lying, but it was sweet that he was lying. Team or not, we both knew that he had done 95% of the work. Our eyes met, and I smiled. "Thank you."

He smiled back. "We must play again sometime."

Mason unceremoniously shoved the pieces into his backpack, slung it over his shoulder, then marched away without saying anything.

Kevin watched him leave. "If you look closely, you can almost see the tail between his legs."

I forced a laugh, suddenly feeling very nervous. This is probably the first time in my life I was alone with Kevin. He was sitting next to me talking to me. In one lesson with Mason, I had gotten further than I had in one year of crushing on — okay, stalking — Kevin.

"Yeah," I said, eyeing Mason's retreating figure with a smile. "What's his deal?"

"He just thinks he's better than everyone," Kevin said simply. "But like most jocks, he'll probably peak in high school. Not like me. Or you."

The bell rang before I could respond.

"Got to go," I said. "We'll play again sometime."

"I'm usually here," Kevin said. He turned back to his game.

I headed towards the school. I pulled out my phone and sent Mason a quick text, thanking him.

Zoe: You didn't have to do that. You didn't have to make yourself look bad.

Mason: Every guy likes to be the knight in shining armor. And knights need dragons to fight. Happy to be your dragon.

Zoe: Can't believe I'm saying this, but you're the best. Your crazy plan worked.

Mason: Sometimes you have to take a hit to make the play.

MASON

I thought about the last text I had sent to Zoe. Sometimes, you had to take a hit to make a play. And at no point was that truer than our first game of the season. It was an absolute slugfest. I stood in the pocket as long as I could before throwing the ball, and it felt like each time I threw, I got crushed. But, somehow, when the clock reached zero, we had won.

Saturday morning, I woke up sore. I spent the morning moving in slow motion, groaning in pain each time I had to do something. Reach for the cereal? Groan. Bend over to put on socks? Groan. Wash my hair in the shower? Groan. Honestly, all I wanted to do was lie on the couch, watch college football, and sleep. But today was supposed to be my first lesson with Zoe. As promised, she was remarkably quiet about what we were supposed to be doing.

The doorbell rang.

I got off the couch, groaning, and opened the front door.

Zoe stood on my front step, a giant smile on her face. She was wearing a cowboy hat, a checkered shirt, and cutoff jean shorts. She had another cowboy hat in her hand, and she shoved it into my chest. "Are y'all ready to go down to the barn to do some dancin'?" She spoke with the most adorable fake Texas drawl.

"Yes ma'am." I put the hat on my head and tipped it. "I'll go wherever you're willing to take me. Should I get my horse out of the garage?"

"That'd be mighty kind of you," Zoe said. "But the place we're going is on High Street, so I think we can wander. Shall we?"

I tipped my hat again, and we were on our way. I was surprised how excited I was to see her.

We fell into easy conversation as we walked.

We talked a bit about the game last night — she came to watch her brother play — and we talked about Life Skills. We decided that our fake people would both be married — not to each other — and would move to Colorado to seek their fame and fortune.

By the time we reached the venue, Zoe had just finished telling me that the top reason to move to Colorado was the altitude. Apparently, the dry mountain air would make her hair a lot easier to control. And, she claimed that due to the thin atmosphere, I'd be able to throw a football further.

I wasn't sure if she was joking.

We stood in front of a small brick building that I'd never noticed. Artistic graffiti covered the walls, showing palm trees, ocean, and shooting stars. Zoe pushed the glass door open and let me inside. The twang of a guitar filled the air.

"I've definitely never been here before," I said.

"That's the least surprising thing I've ever heard," Zoe said. "It's only the best dance studio in Beachbreak. It's where we all go to train over the summer."

"Even Meredith?"

"Especially Meredith." Zoe led me towards the dance studio.

I'd expected a simple room. Some windows, maybe a wooden floor. A stereo sitting in the corner blaring music. What I didn't expect were hay bales, the smell of leather saddles, and a busload of senior citizens. We were the youngest people by decades. Heck, we might've been the only people that had their original hips.

"Did we take a wrong turn?" I asked.

Zoe looked at me innocently. "What? Don't think you can keep up?"

As she spoke, one of the older gentlemen spun his partner around twice, then pulled her into him and dipped her.

"I'm positive that I can't keep up," I said.

"I'll get you there." Zoe took my hand and pulled me to the dance floor.

An older woman with bright blue hair and a plaid shirt pulled away from her partner, and two-stepped over to us. She smiled brightly. "Zoe! I didn't expect to see you today. You know, you're supposed to be above 65 if you want to attend this dance."

"I'm an old soul," Zoe said.

The woman threw back her head and laughed. "You got that right."

Zoe grinned. "Verity, this is my partner for the day — Mason. He wants to learn how to dance, but he's a bit shy. So I thought I would bring him here where he doesn't have to worry about his friends seeing him."

Verity smiled again. "Pleasure to meet you. Any friend of Zoe's is a friend of mine."

I shook her hand. "I'm sorry for what you're about to see."

Verity laughed. "Don't worry about it. Just think — if you start dancing now, imagine how good you'll be when you're my age?"

"Your age? You don't look a day over 20."

Verity swatted my shoulder. "Looks like you found yourself a charmer, Zoe."

Zoe rolled her eyes. "He likes to think he's charming. Let's see if his moves can back up his mouth."

I tipped my hat to Verity. "If you'll excuse me, ma'am, I have a date to attend to."

Zoe rolled her eyes again and pulled me onto the dance floor. She put her hand on my shoulder. "Hold my hand with your right hand and put your other hand on my hip. Perfect. Now, for the two-step, it's simple. Just think of this rhythm in your head: quick, quick, slow, slow."

"Quick, quick, slow, slow," I repeated.

"Since you're the guy, you lead. I get to walk backwards."

"That doesn't seem fair," I said.

"It doesn't, does it?" She laughed and gave my hand a quick squeeze. "But life's not fair. Okay. On three. One, two, three."

I immediately stepped forward with my right foot and stepped on her toe.

She winced and stumbled away.

I blushed. "Sorry — I didn't mean — "

"Lead with your left," Zoe said, grinning.

I looked at my feet. "One, two, three."

This time I lead with my left. I watched her feet, trying to time her movements with mine. Quick, quick, slow, slow. Okay. This wasn't so bad. Maybe I could do this.

"Space Face," Zoe said. "Watch where you're leading me."

I looked up. I was steering us directly into another couple. But, despite knowing that we were on a collision course, I couldn't seem to stop. Quick, quick, slow, slow. "What do I do?" I said, panicking. "How do I make you turn?"

Zoe smiled, and I could tell she was trying to hide a laugh. "Don't overthink it," she said. "Just start moving to the left a little."

I pulled her hips slightly and started moving to the left. Sure enough, we easily avoided the other couple. I went back to looking at my feet.

She squeezed my shoulder. "Word of advice?"

"Yes," I said. "Please give me all the words of advice."

"Dance with your feet, not with your eyes."

"Okay, great," I said, still looking at my feet.

She squeezed my shoulder again. "Look up at me."

"But I'll step on your toes," I said. I couldn't believe how nervous I was about getting this right. I could feel how tense my muscles were. It was easier to stare down a growling linebacker and make a throw then it was to dance. Or at least, a growling linebacker was less terrifying.

"Better to step on my toes while looking in my eyes, than while staring at the floor."

"Fine, but if I break your toes — " My words got lost as I looked into Zoe's eyes. They caught the light and sparkled, and I could see flecks of gold in the green. They reminded me of a summer meadow. Right after a rainstorm.

Zoe smiled warmly. "You're doing good, I promise."

We continued to two-step for two more songs, and I only stepped on her toes three more times. Not once did she stumble. Not once did she make a mistake. The dance was probably simple to her, but she moved with a grace that I could only dream of having.

"Ready to spin me?" Zoe asked.

I took a deep breath and nodded. "Brave of you to put your faith in me."

She grinned. "Don't worry — for the guy, spinning is easy. You just have to time the spin with your steps. But the actual spinning part, you don't have to do anything but raise your hand a little. Like this."

Zoe lifted my hand slightly and spun underneath. She

smoothly came back to me, resting her hand on my shoulder. "Not so bad, hey?"

I was so focused on my steps I didn't realize what happened. "Wait. How did I do that?"

Zoe laughed. "That's the great thing about two-step — you just have to lift your hand and I'm supposed to do the rest."

"Perfect way to learn," I said. "Okay. I'm going to do it. You're going to spin."

She smiled, her eyes sparkling. "Whenever you're ready, cowboy."

Quick, quick, slow, slow, spin.

Zoe spun beneath my arm and pulled up against me again. My hand fell over the familiar curve of her hip. "Not too bad, cowboy. But I got a few more tricks to teach you."

We spent the next hour dancing. She taught me a few more spins — and again, it felt like she was doing 90% of the work. By the end of it, I could dance while looking her in the eye. Occasionally, one of the seniors would recognize her and say something. When they did, she always responded in the most adorable Texas drawl.

I'd never seen this side of her before. I always knew she was dorky — Tyler talked about it constantly. But before today, she'd never been dorky around me.

The last song finished.

"Time's up," Zoe said.

"I guess it is," I said. I was still holding her hand, still resting my other hand on her hip. I spun her once more. Then finally, reluctantly, I released her. "What do you think?"

"You've a bright future. The brightest, even," Zoe said.

"Well, now you're just lying to me."

"It takes practice. Practice leads to confidence, confidence leads to good dancing." Zoe snatched the hat off the top of my head.

"What, do you need that for another student?" There was a slight pang of jealousy in my voice. Where did that come from?

Zoe didn't seem to notice. "I need to bring this back home. If Nina finds out that I gave away her cowboy hat — "

"That was Nina's?"

Zoe smiled innocently. "Couldn't you tell?"

I couldn't tell if she was messing with me or not. We stepped out into the afternoon sun.

"I'll see you Monday," Zoe said.

"See you on Monday."

Still wearing her cowboy hat, Zoe waltzed away. Two passing skateboarders looked at her weirdly, but she just stared back at them, tipped her hat, and continued on her way.

I laughed. Where had Zoe been hiding this part of herself all my life?

ZOE

*M*y chances with Kevin were improving, but only slightly. We didn't have any classes together, so I didn't have any easy opportunities to have a real conversation with him. But at least now he was acknowledging me in the hallway. We'd pass each other, say hi, and then go our separate ways. He probably forgot about me instantly. But for me? This was HUGE.

I couldn't wait to tell Mason about my "progress."

"The problem is we're not exactly part of the same group," I said. It was an overcast Tuesday, and Mason and I were sitting next to each other in Life Skills. "And we don't have any classes together. So I'm not sure what I should do. Or say."

"Having a class together would help," Mason said. "But changing your class schedule to overlap with his would come off as super creepy. And it'll backfire big time if things get awkward."

"Which they will."

"Which they might," Mason corrected. He scribbled down

EMILY LOWRY

an answer on his assignment, then checked it against the textbook.

I'd already finished my assignment. I offered to let him look at my answers, but he refused, which was strange. I'd never had a class with him before, but I had never known Mason to care about school. Wasn't he supposed to take the easy way out in class?

"I don't know what it is," I said. "All I know about him is that he's smart and he likes chess and board games. Which are great, but they're not exactly my hobbies. It feels like we have nothing in common."

"Uh huh," Mason said. "And did you ever wonder why you're so interested in a guy you have nothing in common with?"

"It probably goes back to my childhood," I joked.

Mason smirked.

I looked out the window at the ocean. The waves were rougher than usual today, the water the same grey as the clouds. The world felt colorless. "The only thing I know about dating is you don't get to choose who you like."

"Which would make life so much easier," Mason said. He finished his assignment. "It's not a big deal. You probably do have things in common with him, you just don't know what they are yet."

"And how do I find those out?" I asked. "What's the next step in Mason's Dating for Dummies?"

He shoved the assignment into his binder and clamped the clips closed. "The next move you need to learn is a classic. I call it the 'oh my gosh I accidentally bumped into you when I didn't know you would be here' move."

"If you want your dating class to take off, you're going to need to think of catchier names for your moves," I said.

Mason grinned. "I call it like it is."

"Whatever. So how do I pull this off?"

74

"You start by making yourself pretty with makeup and voodoo and whatever else it is you girls do. You know, the blush and the mascara and the moisturizing sparkle toner." Mason mimed slapping makeup on his face. "Then, you meet me after school on Thursday night, and I'll take you to where Kevin is going to be."

I raised my eyebrows. "And where might that be?"

ZOE

*T*he Night Market at High Street took place every Thursday evening from September to October. Stalls were set up in rows along the beach with fairy lights strung between them. Three food trucks were parked on the sand. These were different each week. Tonight, we had Churro Chums, Something Tasty, and The Pierogi Girls. The smell of sizzling onion and garlic wafted over from the Pierogi Girls truck, and it made my stomach rumble.

I stood, alone at the top of High Street, fidgeting with the hem of my sundress. Someone tapped me on the shoulder.

I spun around. Mason. He looked pretty amazing in a fitted blue t-shirt that brought out the sapphire tones in his ocean eyes. His tousled blond hair flopped on his forehead and he smiled. I grinned back, a little dazed. I'd never had Mason's charm directed at me before.

I was sure he was just trying to show me how it was done.

"What's a nice girl like you doing in a place like this?" He spoke in an accent right out of a forties movie.

I played along, infusing my mannerisms with extra daintiness. "Why, I took a wrong turn and ended up here. And now I'm hopelessly lost without a gentleman to save me. Now, I don't see any gentlemen around, but perhaps you'll do?"

Mason laughed. "Have you eaten?"

My stomach growled in response.

"Let's find you some food before you eat me," Mason said. We lined up for Pierogi Girls and ordered.

"You don't have to pay," I said, pulling out my wallet.

It was too late — he'd already handed a twenty to the girl behind the counter. "You'll need your money for later."

"Oh?"

Mason winked. "You'll see."

We ate our pierogies while wandering through the Night Market. I kept catching girls stealing glances at Mason and then looking at me with… jealousy? This was a whole new sensation for me. Nobody was ever jealous of me. I peeked at Mason, who seemed oblivious to all the attention he was getting.

We explored the stores as we went. My favorite shop was a striped tent called "All That Glitters." It sold incredibly garish fake jewelry. There were fake rubies the size of my knuckle, a "diamond" necklace with baubles bigger than my fist, and a crown with sapphire points. Mason put the crown on and started demanding that random passersby pledged allegiance to the King of the Night Market. To my surprise, some did. It was amazing how far blind confidence could take you.

Next, we went to a wooden stand that featured a muscular man and a woman in a bikini. There were little holes you could put your face in to get your picture taken. Naturally, Mason pretended to be the woman in the bikini, and I was the Venice Beach bodybuilder.

We had just finished buying a bag of saltwater taffy when Mason announced the next part of his plan.

"We're doing a context switch. Fancy words — I had to look them up," Mason joked.

"A context switch?"

He tied a twist tie around the bag of taffy. "Right now, Kevin only knows you as a girl who goes to his school. You've never talked to him outside of school. When you constantly see the same person in the same place, you put them in a box. And you don't think they could ever be more than that. Think about how weird it is when you see a teacher outside of school."

I thought about my recent run-in with Mr. Hinshaw and his wife on High Street. They were antiquing, he told me. And even weirder — he looked legitimately happy. Since that moment, he'd been nicer to me in Physics class, and I couldn't figure out why. Maybe the context switch thingy Mason was talking about had happened. And worked. "Okay," I said. "I'll buy that."

"So what you need to do is get him to see you as not just another student," he said. "Which is why I told you to dress up all pretty tonight. By the way — mission accomplished."

"Thanks." I blushed. Mason didn't really think I was pretty — he was just trying to be nice and psych me up before whatever it was he had planned. "So, where's Kevin supposed to be?"

Mason puffed up his chest. "You should be proud — I used all my detective skills for this one. And by that, I mean I checked their website."

"Whose website?"

"Sand and Sun Board Games." Mason pointed to the end of the aisle of stalls, and sure enough, there was a small booth with board games. Kevin was inside the booth, adjusting the angle of a board game so it stood out to anyone walking by.

And, as usual when Kevin appeared in my life, I was immediately nervous. I took a deep breath. "What do I say?"

"You could start with something like 'Hey Kevin' — something simple," Mason said. Was he making fun of me?

I rolled my eyes. "Clever. Real memorable."

"Maybe tell him you didn't know he worked there."

"But I did know."

"Yeah, not the point," Mason said. "Guys like to help. Tell him you're thinking about getting into the hobby and that you need an intro level board game. Tell him you're tired of Monopoly."

"At least that's true," I said. "I am tired of Monopoly."

"You and everyone else," Mason replied. "He'll probably bring up something simple like Settlers of Catan or Ticket to Ride."

I eyed Mason suspiciously. "Since when do you know about board games?"

"Since I became your dating coach," Mason said.

I was impressed. He was putting more effort into my dating life than I was. I took another look at Kevin.

He hadn't spotted me yet.

"Okay," I said. "I can do this. I'm not nervous, I'm not nervous…"

Mason put his hand on my shoulder. His touch sent a shiver down my spine. "It's okay to be nervous. I'm always nervous before the game starts. You just gotta feel it and do it anyway."

I nodded. "Okay. I'm going."

The walk to Kevin's tent felt like it took forever. I kept waiting for him to look up and notice me, but he was too busy adjusting various board games. A perfectionist, I figured. I could admire that kind of dedication. Finally, I was at the stall.

He still hadn't noticed me.

"Hi, Kevin." My voice squeaked like it came from a cartoon mouse.

Kevin looked at me, surprised, then smiled. "Zoe! How can I help you?"

I pretended to look at the various board games. The boxes were loud and colorful, almost overwhelming. "I was thinking about getting into board games," I said. "I was wondering if you have any recommendations? Something easy to learn?"

"Right this way," Kevin said enthusiastically. He guided me towards a shelf. "I'm always happy to get someone into the hobby."

"Great," I said. "I'm all yours."

I was doing it.

I was actually talking to a guy I liked.

Now I just had to not blow it.

MASON

I hung out in a stall that was about twenty yards away from Kevin's. The Night Market was crowded enough that they wouldn't see me, and it gave me the opportunity to casually spy so I could think of things that Zoe could improve for next time. That's all I was doing, wasn't it? Just watching so I could help?

Zoe laughed at something. When she laughed — like really laughed — she threw her head back and ran her fingers through her hair, almost pulling it. It was quickly becoming one of my favorite sights — and sounds — in the world. It was such a carefree, relaxed laugh.

Kevin handed her a board game.

Her brow furrowed as she examined the box, flipping it over. The glow from the fairy lights caught her skin just the right way, seeming to highlight the soft curves of her face. There must have been hundreds of other people at the Night Market, but my eyes were drawn to her. She was the best kind of beautiful — the kind of beautiful that didn't know she was beautiful.

Kevin, on the other hand? Dull as a practice jersey. Why

was Zoe so nervous around him? If anything, he should've been nervous around her. She was that far out of his league.

Or maybe I was just being hard on him. Just because I didn't think chess or board games were that interesting, didn't mean they weren't. There was nothing wrong with having interests besides sports. Besides, Kevin was smarter than me. I was just your typical high school jock.

But as I looked at Zoe, I just didn't get how a guy like Kevin wouldn't be interested in Zoe. For that matter, I couldn't understand how any guy wouldn't be interested in Zoe.

21

ZOE

I bounced back to Mason, a paper bag dangling by my side. Inside the bag was my newest board game. I pulled it out and presented it to him. "I'm now the proud owner of 'The Quest for El Dorado.' It's an adventure game, apparently. You're an explorer and you have to journey across the jungle to find some gold."

"This actually looks kind of cool." Mason examined the brightly-colored box and traced his finger along the outline of a golden statue. "How'd the whole flirting thing go?"

"He was so nice and polite. Funny, too," I said. I wasn't sure if I imagined it or not, but it looked like Mason's smile flickered ever so slightly. "I think I did okay."

"I'm sure you were great," Mason said. His voice sounded... almost jealous?

No. That couldn't be right, could it?

But, as our adventure through the Night Market continued, I couldn't deny that Mason seemed off. We checked out a few more booths, and while he continued to crack jokes, he wasn't able to muster the same enthusiasm he had before I'd awkwardly flirted with Kevin. I was probably just reading too much into everything. Maybe he was tired. Probably, he was tired.

Tired of hanging out with me. Being my coach. That was it. Mason had better things to do on a Thursday night, I was sure.

While he was busy chatting with a vendor about a present for his sister's birthday, I wandered to the information booth.

Kenzie, the overachiever that she was, was on volunteer duty tonight. She saw me and smiled. "Zoe! You should've told me you were coming! I could've got you… well, we don't really do discounts… I could've… the point is, you should've told me. What are you doing here?"

"I'm with Mason," I said.

Kenzie's eyes widened. "Alone?"

"It's date training," I said.

She glanced at the logo on my paper bag. "I see you've already found Prince Boring. How'd it go?"

"He's not boring," I said. "We just don't have much in common. And it went well, I think. I didn't swallow my tongue and I didn't spill anything on him, so it was probably the best flirting I've ever done."

Kenzie snorted. "Impressive. Truly. What do you have planned next?"

"Cheering up Mason, I think," I said. He was still bartering with the vendor. I turned back to Kenzie. "Do you have any ideas?"

Kenzie grinned mischievously. "Oh, I have the perfect thing for you two."

MASON

I bought a stuffed frog for Chelsey. It had a voice box inside, and a voice recorder. When you squeezed the frog, it talked. I recorded a quick message, then, when I was sure Zoe wasn't looking, I bought something else. I didn't know when it would come in handy — maybe it could be a reward for her first date with Kevin? — but I had it if I needed it.

I made sure the stuffed frog was in the top of the bag, then made my way over to where Zoe and Kenzie were chatting.

Kenzie looked up, and her cheeks reddened.

"Hi, Mason." She tucked a strand of dark hair behind her ear.

"What's up, Kenz?" I grinned.

Before she could answer, Zoe spun. "We're leaving the bags here. I have somewhere to take you."

I hesitated. Honestly, I'd been thinking of heading home. I had a game tomorrow night, and I couldn't shake the image of her laughing with Kevin. That was the whole point of our

"Mason's Dating for Dummies" classes, but it didn't sit right. It was like I'd eaten a sandwich from a gas station. It probably wouldn't kill me, but I didn't like the way it made me feel.

Zoe frowned slightly. "You okay?"

"I…"

She waited, her excitement fading slightly. I couldn't let that happen.

I looked at Kenzie. "We can leave these here?"

"Yep!" Zoe snatched my bag and practically threw it towards Kenzie. Then she grabbed my hand and pulled me through the Night Market. Booths blurred as we jogged through the crowd. Zoe moved like a running back — a graceful one. She juked and spun through the crowd, pulling me towards the shore.

Specifically, she was pulling me towards the docks, which were lined with tiki torches.

And there was something else.

Something that made my jaw drop.

"Are you kidding?" I asked.

"It's amazing, right?"

At the end of the dock, there was a dance floor. Not just any dance floor — a floating dance floor on what I assumed was a pontoon. The floor was made of tiles that lit up in different colors, and there was a DJ booth in one corner. The DJ was an old man in a pressed suit. Gold glasses sat on his hooked nose, and he was playing music on vinyl.

Couples — mostly middle-aged or older — whirled around the dance floor to the upbeat music.

"Is this swing?" I asked.

"Jive," Zoe said.

"There's a difference?"

"Absolutely," Zoe said, her eyes lighting up. "Same family,

but swing has a lot more twisting. Jive is bouncier. Are you ready?"

When she looked at me like that, with her eyes sparkling, how could I say no? I didn't wait for her to lead the way. Instead, I barreled down the steps, pulling her behind me. I lead her to the center of the crowded dance floor.

"Now what?" I asked.

"Give me your hands."

I did.

"Now watch my feet."

I couldn't hear her over the music. "What?"

She leaned in close enough for me to smell her perfume. Vanilla and cinnamon. When she spoke, her lips were near my ear and I felt her breath on my cheek. "Watch my feet. Mirror my moves."

I took her hands and watched her feet.

"This is a rock step," she said. She moved one foot behind the other, putting her weight on her back foot. "Then you transition into a triple step, like this. You try."

I tried.

She winked. "A natural."

"I doubt it."

"You'll get there. Let's try to the music."

I wasn't the best dancer — not by a mile. But with Zoe's instructions, I could jive somewhat in time to the music without making a complete fool of myself. Our knees only knocked together once or twice, at which point she told me to angle my hips slightly.

It was amazing how different Zoe was once you got her on the dance floor. She moved with complete confidence, in perfect rhythm with the music. She was also kind and encouraging, even when I accidentally bumped into her — or sent her spinning into other people. Not that that happened often — she was a good enough dancer that she just adjusted her footwork, avoided them, and made everything look intentional.

Somehow, she was making me look good.

23

ZOE

*M*agic.

That was the only way I could describe my night. The music, the stars, the colorful lights, and Mason's hands in mine. I had a curfew, but I did not care what time it was. There was no way I was going home. Not until they forced us off the floating dance floor.

Mason spun me, then pulled me close, catching me in his arms, and dipping me to the floor.

I let my hair fall back and laughed.

He lifted me back up to him. "How am I doing?"

The way he smiled made me shiver in the warmest way. I grinned. "I think you're ready for the next move. It's called the octopus."

Mason let out an exaggerated gasp. "You're throwing me to an octopus?"

I laughed again and rolled my eyes. "It'd probably just throw you back."

"Be careful," he warned playfully, "or I'll spin you right off the dance floor."

"Put your money where your mouth is, Space Face. Move

your hand like this and do a rock step." I made a semicircle with my hand. On our next rock step, he repeated the gesture.

Then the spinning started.

I spun — slowly, just in case — under his arm, spinning in front of him. In theory, we would've performed this perfectly, and he would've repeated the spin, spinning in front of me this time. In practice, we became a stumbling tangle of limbs.

"How are your hands on my legs?" I asked, trying to control my laughter.

"I thought it made sense?"

"Not even a little bit," I sputtered. "Here. Try again."

We tried again.

This time, we did better, our bodies slightly less of a tangled mess. The third time wasn't quite the charm, but there was definite improvement. By the time we had it mastered, Mason's face was a frown of concentration, and I suspected he was mildly dizzy.

"Look at you, Mr. Focus," I said. "I've never seen anyone looking like they're concentrating harder. You need to relax. Like ninety percent of dancing is in your cheeks." With my fingers, I mimed pushing my cheeks up into a smile.

Mason spun me again. "All this time, I thought you were supposed to use your feet to dance."

"Nope," I said. "It's all in your face."

"Like this?" Mason puffed his cheeks out like he was a blowfish. A stupid, grinning blowfish.

I smiled. "Exactly."

He spun me.

When I faced him once more, he'd changed his facial expression. Now, instead of a blowfish, he sucked his cheeks in and puffed his lips out like a guppy.

Laughter bubbled in my chest. If he was going to keep

making faces, I was going to have a tough time keeping control — and when you danced, control was everything.

We did the octopus.

Then he dipped me, and when he dipped me, his face changed once more. He sucked his lips in like he was an old man and furrowed his brow. When he spoke, he sounded like my grandpa. "Oh, my back."

He bent over and clutched his back. Then, a mischievous grin on his face, he mimed grabbing a walker and dancing with it. He even pretended to spin it, then made a show out of lunging for it when it didn't come back.

I lost control, laughing so hard that tears blurred my eyes.

Unfortunately, this only encouraged Mason's ridiculousness. Now, his facial expression was changing into something new and absurd every three seconds. He went from old man, to robot, to Frankenstein's Monster, to Frankenstein's Monster doing the robot, to what I thought was a zombie.

Meanwhile, I couldn't breathe due to my laughter so I practically crawled off the dance floor. I grabbed the railing and looked back at Mason.

He. Was. A. Spectacle.

Not just to me. The other dancers had also noticed what was going on. Some cheered him on. Others laughed. And one older woman that I recognized even joined in.

Verity slid up beside Mason and mirrored his moves. They pretended to be shopping together, reaching for items on the shelf, checking them, and putting them in the shopping cart. At one point, apparently, they bought a sprinkler. And then, completely out of time with the music, Mason started doing the macarena.

That was too much for Verity, who also burst out laughing. Doubled over, she found her way to me.

Mason was still dancing — now with Verity's husband.

They looked like they were trying to perform Riverdance. They finished, grabbed each other's hands, and jived.

"My goodness, that boy is learning," Verity said.

My lungs hurt from laughing. "Looks like."

Mason tried to lead Verity's husband into the octopus. Unfortunately, neither of them knew the woman's part, so it ended with Mason getting elbowed in the face. It didn't deter him at all — it only caused him and Verity's husband to break down in wild laughter.

Verity placed her hand on my shoulder and smiled. "That boy is an absolute treasure."

I smiled back. Mason was a treasure. And even if he wasn't my treasure, I was thrilled for whoever he was going to end up with.

24

ZOE

Under Mason's guidance, both my dating life and my social life were slowly but surely improving. Kevin moved beyond simply nodding at me in the hallway — now we had five-minute chats about whatever board game he was interested in. There was a lot of smiling and nodding dumbly on my part, but still — progress!

Meanwhile, Mason had started making funny faces every time he saw me talking to Kevin. Rumors swirled about why the gorgeous high school quarterback couldn't keep a straight face — ever. I warned him that he needed to be careful or his face might stay like that. He told me he hoped it did, because he needed a challenge.

Physics was still a struggle, but I was managing a solid B. I usually tested well, so I hoped that when finals rolled around in December, I could bump my mark up.

However, despite the improvements in my social life, when Saturday night rolled around, I was still planning to spend it the same way I always did — alone. Or at least, I'd be alone as soon as Tyler and Mason left for the beach party at Highline Hideaway.

We were all hanging out in the kitchen. Mason and my brother were both dressed for a night out— new jeans, crisp t-shirts just tight enough to show off their muscles. I, meanwhile, was dressed for a night in — old gray sweatpants, hoodie, messy ponytail. Perfect for the Netflix binge awaiting me.

Tyler's phone vibrated. He opened the message and his eyebrows rose so high I thought they'd leave his forehead. Then, his face relaxed into a huge, ear-splitting smile.

"That's a suspicious grin if I've ever seen one," I said.

"It's her," Tyler replied.

"I don't know how you can date that she-demon."

"You should be supportive," Tyler said.

Okay. That was fair. I hadn't been supportive of my brother's burgeoning situationship with Parker — but that's only because I knew the real Parker, while Ty just liked her pretty, popular mask. But under that sweetness-and-light façade, Parker was an entirely different person. She'd been one of Nina's best friends in middle school. Then, almost overnight, she turned on Nina. Nina didn't know why and pretended not to care. But I'd never forgiven her.

"I'll try to be neutral," I said. It was as big of a concession as I could make.

"Is Parker coming to Hideaway?" Mason asked.

Tyler shook his head. "She wants to meet me on High Street. Just the two of us."

"Like a date?"

"Yeah." Tyler's smile faded. "It's all good, dude. I'll tell her I've already got plans with you. Maybe she'll come to Hideaway."

"No way, man," Mason said instantly. "This is your chance to go out with the girl you've been crushing on. Don't let me get in your way. There'll be other parties."

"Nah, I don't want to ditch you."

"I'll keep him entertained," I blurted.

Tyler snorted. "I'm definitely not ditching you with my little sister."

"Very funny," I said sarcastically, crossing my arms. "It's not like I have any plans. And he could probably use another dancing lesson. His footwork is still…"

Mason frowned. "You said my footwork was good."

"My toes are still sore from our last dance." I winked. Mason's footwork was good — surprisingly good. He was a natural athlete, and, as he explained it to me, a lot of quarter-backing relied on proper footwork. I smiled at my brother. "Seriously. I'll keep him company so you don't feel like you're ditching him. So go. Go on your date with… her. This is the most supportive I'll ever be."

"Are you sure?" Tyler asked. "Are you both sure?"

Mason and I responded simultaneously. "Go."

My brother left the house so fast he left a Tyler-shaped hole in the wall. Mom was also gone for the evening, at an open house. Which meant Mason and I were alone.

The idea didn't make me feel nearly as nervous as I expected. If anything, I was excited. At least now I had some-thing to do on a Saturday night.

"You really don't have to entertain me," Mason said. "I can still hit Hideaway. All the guys from the team will be there."

I bit the inside of my cheek. Was he being polite, or did he actually want to do something else? Something without me? "You can stay, too," I said. "I was just going to melt into the couch and watch some cheesy movies. Or a trashy reality show. Haven't decided which."

"You should watch them in the treehouse like we used to when we were kids."

I looked out the kitchen window. Our treehouse was perched in an old eucalyptus tree in the backyard. My uncle built it for Tyler and I years ago. When we were kids, we loved it. We had sleepovers there every weekend. Sometimes it was just me and Ty, sometimes all three of us, and sometimes four, if Nina was over. We devoured popcorn, chips, soda, and movies. Sometimes, we watched movies until the sun rose, but most of the time, we fell asleep through the third or fourth film.

"I don't even remember the last time I was in the treehouse," I said.

"Feels like forever," Mason said. He nodded to himself, his expression resolute. "We should do it."

"Do what?"

"A treehouse movie night. Get some popcorn, some snacks, and set up your laptop in the treehouse. Then watch a bunch of movies. Just like when we were kids." Mason opened the refrigerator. "We can head over to High Street and grab everything we need. My treat."

Was this actually happening? Mason was picking me over a party at Hideaway?

I imagined spending the night watching movies in the treehouse with Mason. Visions of snuggling up to him flew through my head, completely uninvited.

My stomach flipped.

Calm down, Zoe. It's Mason. He wants to revisit childhood memories. Childhood. No snuggling involved.

We walked to Highstreet to grab snacks: cheese popcorn, salt and vinegar chips, sour candy, and Highline Soda — Root Beer for Mason, Blueberry Blast for me. I rummaged through our storage room and pulled out our old sleeping bags. They smelled musty, but they would work. Before I knew it, I was climbing the rickety wooden ladder to the tree house.

"If I fall, you better catch me," I shouted over my shoulder.

"No promises," Mason said. I could practically hear his smirk.

The treehouse was different than I remembered it. Smaller, somehow. There was a tiny table, which we used to play cards on, and then a raised bench in the corner that was just large enough to squeeze in two sleeping bags. I set my laptop on the table.

Mason climbed into the treehouse. He bumped his head and winced. "I think this place has shrunk."

"No," I said, "your head has expanded so it could fit your massive ego, and now you can't stop bumping it on things."

Smiling, Mason unfurled the sleeping bags. "You're probably right."

I poured our snacks into giant plastic bowls, then set up the laptop. "Our first movie is 'It Came from Beneath the Stairs.' The remake, not the original."

"Opening with a horror movie?"

I climbed inside my sleeping bag, careful not to disturb the snacks. "Just like when we were kids. We'll alternate between horror movies and romantic comedies. The cheesier the better."

"I wonder what's cheesier: a really bad horror movie, or a really bad romantic comedy?"

I shrugged. "Dunno. Either way, we'll be cringing a lot."

I was right. Our horror movie opened with a scantily clad teenager hearing a thump in the basement. She went to investigate, and sure enough, that was the end of her screen time.

"Just like the original," Mason said. He shoved a handful of popcorn into his mouth.

"You remember the original?"

"We watched it when we were kids."

"Back when everything was simple," I said.

Mason laughed. "Remember the types of problems we'd have when we were eight or nine?"

"Mom made me eat broccoli," I whined playfully.

"I don't want to go to bed — I'm not tired!"

"My bike isn't as fast as Tyler's."

Mason bumped me with his shoulder. "Maybe you were just slow?"

I bumped him back. "Says the boy who never tried to ride a bike in his Sunday dress."

"You don't know that. Maybe I did try to ride my bike while wearing my dress."

I laughed. "Yes, I distinctly remember you in your frilly Sunday dress. Rose print, was it?"

"Lilacs," Mason said, grinning. "Now stop bumping me. You're spilling the popcorn."

I bumped him once more for good measure. When I thought about it, it was amazing how different life was back then. How different it was now. If life could change that much in a few years, how different would it look five years from now? Ten years from now?

"What're you going to do after school?" I asked.

"According to Life Skills, I'm moving to Colorado to become a radio personality," Mason said.

"And not according to Life Skills?"

Mason twisted the top off a soda bottle and took a drink. "I've got a football scholarship to UCLA."

He said this with all the excitement of someone reporting on tomorrow's weather.

"Are you going to take it?"

"Dad'll kill me if I don't," he said. He opened his mouth to say something, then clamped his lips shut.

"But…?"

He sighed. "But I don't know if I'm smart enough for college."

My brow furrowed. He looked… serious. Did he actually not think he was smart enough? Sure, Mason wasn't on the Honor Roll, but he was a decent student. "You're smart," I said. "You get good marks."

"I don't know if I'd call them good," he said. "Let's settle for above average. But that's beside the point. I'm the starting quarterback, and I only get above average marks. If you're on the football team and your grades fall too far, they don't let you play. And let's face it — our school is big into football."

I waited.

Mason stared at the movie. "It's such a cliché, but I know that regular rules don't apply to me. If I skip class, the teachers ignore it so I can still play. It seems like it would be awesome, but any time I get a mark back on something, I wonder whether I got a good mark because I deserved it, or…"

"Or whether they're giving you a good mark so you can play."

"Exactly," he said. "Hard to know if you're actually smart when everyone is bending over backwards to prove you're smart."

Instinctively, I squeezed his hand. "I think you're smart. Look at everything you did to set me up with Kevin. If nothing else, you could be a private detective."

"Solving dating mysteries for girls everywhere," Mason joked.

"If you can figure me out, you can figure out anything," I said.

He squeezed my hand. "You're not as awkward as you think. How are things going with Kevin?"

"I'm not sure," I said. "I think they're going well? But I've thought that before, then — boom. Everything goes pear-shaped. That's what it always does when I like a guy."

"Not this time," Mason said. "Not with me as your sidekick. But even if it does, it's not a big deal. You're still awesome. You'll find someone."

"It's not that simple," I said. It was never that simple. "My parents met in college. Love at first sight, or something like that. And despite the divorce, my mom keeps telling me that college is the best time to meet someone. Don't worry about meeting boys in high school, she says. College boys are way better. Way smarter. But I know that if I don't have any experience dating before college, even if I do meet the one, I'll just blow it."

Mason didn't reply.

That was probably for the best, as I wasn't done. "And what if the world's like that? What if there is only one person you're supposed to be with? And what if I meet that one person in college, and I screw it up because I don't have any experience? Then what? I live alone with my cats?"

There it was. All of my insecurities laid bare. The truth that I had known for a long time was that it was never about Kevin. Yes, I had a crush on him. A crush I'd had since forever. But it was so much bigger than him. I needed to know that I could do this. I needed to know that if I liked a boy, I could get him to date me.

"You probably think it's stupid," I said.

"It's not stupid," Mason whispered. "And I'm sure that if there is one person for everyone, your one is going to be pretty understanding. He's going to be amazing, too."

"That's easy for you to say. You've dated before. You know what you're doing — I don't even know how to kiss."

Mason shrugged, still staring straight ahead at the laptop. "You can learn how to kiss. Heck, I could teach you how to kiss."

My heart practically stopped. Suddenly, I was hyper aware of everything around me. The warmth of Mason's hand, his fingers entwined with mine. The scent of his body, fresh laundry and ocean salt and sunscreen. How handsome he looked in the darkness. "You would teach me how to kiss?"

"If you want to know," he said casually.

Of course I wanted to know. I tried to keep my voice steady and prevent my hands from trembling. "Sure, if you'll teach me," I said, trying to match the casualness in his voice.

We both sat up.

His eyes met mine with an unusual intensity. They were exceptionally blue in this light. "When you kiss someone, it's not about being fancy. There's no trick to it. Just think of it as an expression of how much you like someone."

My hands were still trembling with a nervous energy, so I folded them in my lap. "I'm going to need more than that," I said. "Do I lick my lips? Put my tongue in their mouth? Ooh, or bite their lip? I heard that's a thing."

"For your first kiss, I'd recommend trying exactly none of the above." Mason grinned. "You're getting ahead of yourself. The key is to take it slow. The best part of the kiss is the anticipation. There's this sweet spot, when you know you're about to kiss, but you haven't actually kissed yet."

"And how am I supposed to know when that's happening?"

"Because he'll do something like this." Mason brushed my hair away from my eyes, but left his hand on my cheek. His touch felt like an electric shock. "If a guy touches your face, that means he wants to kiss you. So if you don't want to kiss him back, this is when you pull away, turn your head, or tell him he's got food in his teeth."

"Spinach in his teeth, got it." My heart was beating so loudly I was sure Mason could hear it.

"You need to watch his eyes," Mason said. His eyes were locked with mine, a perfect blend of ocean blues and greens.

"His eyes will move to your lips. Just a quick glance. Just like this."

Mason's gaze flickered from my eyes, to my lips, then back to my eyes.

My stomach flipped. Why was I suddenly finding it so hard to breathe? And was it hot in here?

"Okay," I croaked. "What's next?"

"You do the same thing," Mason said. "Glance at his lips. Just for a heartbeat. If he knows what he's doing, he'll know this means you want to kiss him."

"I didn't think there'd be so much science involved," I said.

Mason smiled. "It's chemistry, isn't it?"

"Clever," I said. I glanced at Mason's lips. They looked soft, and I had the almost insatiable urge to press my mouth against his. I resisted.

"Then you both lean in."

Mason leaned in slowly.

I leaned towards him.

"You need to close your eyes," Mason said as his face came close to mine. "Close your eyes just before your noses touch."

His nose brushed against mine, and I closed my eyes. I felt the heat from his face, and I tasted his scent. Warm, fresh, earthy. Like a summer day in a forest. At that moment, I wanted to kiss him so badly it almost hurt.

"Tilt your head, like this," Mason whispered.

I felt something rough on my lips. Not soft, like I expected his mouth to feel. Startled, I open my eyes.

Mason was still there, his face next to mine. But our lips weren't touching. He'd cleverly positioned his thumb in the space between our mouths.

I had the urge to bite his thumb just so he would move it, just so I could feel his mouth on mine, but before I gave in, he pulled away.

"Obviously, you won't put your thumb in the way," he said. "I just did it because you should save your actual first kiss for someone you care about."

My breath caught in my throat. "How long is a kiss supposed to last?"

"Just long enough to feel like you want a bit more," Mason said.

I already knew exactly what that felt like.

25

ZOE

*S*unlight filtered through the window, burning my face.

I wished someone would close the curtains. I rubbed my eyes and squinted against the sunlight. What happened last night? Why was I in my sleeping bag in the treehouse? And what was that steady thumping noise?

The night came rushing back to me. Our decision to watch movies in the treehouse. Our talks about what we wanted for our futures.

Our almost kiss.

And now, my sleeping bag was curled against his, my head resting on his chest, listening to his steady heartbeat. We must have fallen asleep in the middle of the night and, when we were both asleep, I rolled over and accidentally cuddled against him. It was an easy mistake to make. The treehouse was cramped, after all.

The excuse didn't stop the heat from rising to my cheeks.

I pulled away from Mason and prayed that I hadn't left a drool stain on his t-shirt. The fabric was clean, thank goodness. It would be the ultimate Zoe move to literally drool on the guy I liked.

Whoa.

The guy I liked?

No, that wasn't right.

I liked Kevin.

Kevin.

K-E-V-I-N.

That was the whole point in spending time with Mason, wasn't it? So I could get closer to Mason?

NO.

Not so I could get closer to Mason.

So I could get closer to Kevin.

KEVIN.

"I'm a disaster," I mumbled.

Mason yawned. He opened his eyes, saw me, and jumped backwards.

I winced. I must've been a sight to see first thing in the morning. No makeup. My hair pointing out at weird angles. And — the worst part — morning breath. I made a mental note to cover my mouth whenever I spoke. "I know I'm not the hottest girl at school, but I like to think boys don't jump with fright when they see me."

Mason chuckled. "It's not that. I'm not used to waking up next to someone. And trust me, it's not your looks. The sunlight's giving you a bit of a halo right now. Like an angel."

"Smooth recovery, Space Face."

"I thought so," Mason said. He sat up and stretched, the hem of his shirt lifting just enough to see his abs. He swore. "Did we stay out here all night? Does anyone know?"

"Let's hope not," I said. Tyler would never let either of us live it down if he caught us accidentally — and it was an accident — cuddling in the treehouse. And mom? She would ground me for life for spending a night with a boy. Even if it was just Mason. "I guess there's only one way to find out."

"I'll lead the way," Mason said. "Take the hit if I need to."

"It was both of our faults," I said.

Nervously, we descended the ladder and headed towards the house. I peeked inside the patio door, but everything was dark. Tyler probably crashed at a friend's, and Mom must've been out running errands. Upstairs, my bedroom door was still closed.

"They probably came home and thought I was sleeping in my room," I said.

"So our secret's safe?"

"Our secret's safe," I agreed.

Mason let out a relieved sigh. "Now that that's off our minds, you have any plans today?"

"Physics homework."

"You sound really excited."

"So, so, excited," I said sarcastically. "Why enjoy your youth when you can lock yourself in a room and review formulas?"

Mason smiled and ran his hands through his hair. "Well, if you're looking for a distraction…"

"Please," I said. "Distract me."

"How do you feel about breakfast?"

My stomach growled in agreement.

I dug around in the medicine cabinet and hurled a new toothbrush at Mason, before I fled to my bedroom. After a quick makeup application, hairbrush and scrubbing away of my morning breath, I changed into jean shorts and an off the shoulder top.

Before heading back downstairs, I checked my reflection in the mirror. Twice.

What was happening to me? Since when did I care what Mason thought?

We went to High Street to feast. It was Sunday morning, and the cafés were packed with people. We stood in line for a half hour to get toasted bagels smeared with avocado, a slice of tomato, and two strips of bacon, along with freshly-made oat milk flat whites — the latest coffee craze in Beachbreak.

Rather than stuff ourselves into one of the tiny tables, we walked across the street and curled our toes in the sand as we strolled along the beach, the morning surf splashing against our ankles. We chatted a bit, but mostly we just walked together in a companionable silence. Being alone with Mason was starting to feel like the most natural thing in the world.

He took a sip of his coffee and eyed the waves. "Feels like a beach day, doesn't it?"

"I could do a beach day," I said.

26

MASON

$\mathcal{A}$s I jogged home to get my stuff for our beach day, I couldn't get Zoe out of my head. I changed into my swim shorts, shoved a towel in my backpack, and briefly considered bringing her surprise present from the Night Market before deciding against it. I'd save that for later, for just the right time.

Zoe had the type of personality that made you miss her, even when she was right next to you — which was why I was so excited to have her to myself on a beautiful Sunday afternoon.

I met her on the beach at Highline Hideaway. It was still early enough that it wasn't packed with kids from school yet. I had Zoe all to myself.

She was standing next to her deflated unicorn. She smiled at me, then nudged the unicorn with her toes. "You're full of hot air. Why don't you blow him up?"

"Me? Hot air? Never." I popped the cap off the spout, filled my lungs, and breathed life into Sparkles. When I was done, we put him in the water.

Zoe set a cooler on the inflatable unicorn, then we both

hopped on. There was just enough room for the two of us. Which was good. Because suddenly, I was all too aware of just how cute she looked in her baby blue one-piece bathing suit.

"Where to?" I asked.

Zoe eyed the cove like she was looking for something. Or someone.

Kevin?

She shrugged. "Let's get away from here. Have you ever been around the bend?"

"No. You?"

"Nope. You up for an adventure?"

"Definitely." I slid my feet into the water and kicked, directing us around the bend on the south side of Hideaway. The golden beach gave way to lush green forest, and soon, the excited shouts and chatter of Hideaway were out of earshot. I climbed back onto Sparkles.

Zoe eyed the sun and sighed. "I forgot to put on sunscreen."

"Scared of getting a tan?"

"I don't tan. I don't even burn. I blister." She dug in her cooler and pulled out a tube of sunscreen. She hesitated. "Umm... would you... mind?"

"No problem," I said. My voice almost cracked.

She passed me the tube of sunscreen and then turned her back to me.

I squirted the lotion into my hand, then rubbed my palms together to warm it up. My heart beat quickly. "Ready?"

I wasn't sure if I was asking her or myself.

27

ZOE

*M*y heart was pounding in my chest, my hands shaking slightly. I reached back and pulled my hair to the side. "Ready whenever you are."

Mason placed his hands on my shoulders and rubbed in the lotion. His hands were the perfect kind of rough, just enough to create friction. They were strong, too, and as he rubbed the lotion onto my back, my muscles relaxed. The smell of coconut mingled with the fresh sea air and the spray of saltwater. The only sound was the waves lapping against Sparkles.

"Done," Mason said, pulling his hands away.

I almost fell backwards into him — I hadn't realized how hard I was leaning against his hands. My cheeks felt hot, and I had the sudden urge to leap into the ocean to cool down.

"Thanks," I said, choosing to lie on my stomach, my face tilted away from him. I'd been to the beach with Mason a million times. Seen him shirtless, in his swim shorts. Why was this so different?

We drifted lazily around the bend, away from Hideaway. Away from everything but the forest. Out here, it felt like we were the only people in the world. And I was definitely okay with that.

The tide pulled us around the bend to another, smaller cove I'd never seen before. There was a sandy beach littered with seashells. It was only big enough for four, maybe five people. A rope hammock was strung up, shaded by a pair of trees.

"Do you see it?" I asked, pointing to the beach.

"Looks like a good place for a picnic."

"Exactly what I was thinking," I said.

"Allow me, Cap'n." Mason rolled off the raft and dove into the water. He floated above the surface, his wet skin shimmering in the sun, and slicked his hair back. Then he grabbed Sparkles around the neck, and, floating on his back, kicked, pulling us to shore.

I hopped off Sparkles.

Cool water enveloped my legs. The sand beneath my toes was smooth as silk.

We dragged Sparkles onto the shore and sat him in the hammock.

"He could use a break," I said.

"Me too." Mason pretended to be out of breath.

"Big tough football player can't handle a little swim?"

"Nah, I just wanted the hammock."

I laughed. "You won't want the hammock when you see what I've got in store for us. I present... our lunch."

Lunch was sliced strawberries, a tub of blueberries, two ham and swiss croissants, and leftover popcorn and candy.

Mason eyed the popcorn suspiciously. "Didn't we forget to close the bag? Isn't it stale?"

"Popcorn's better when it's stale," I said, taking a giant handful.

Mason laughed like I was joking.

But I wasn't. Popcorn WAS better when it was just a little

stale. It was softer. Almost chewy. Especially if you soaked it in butter, which I normally did.

"You're weird, Zoo," Mason said. "The best kind of weird. But still weird."

"Takes one to know one."

On our own private beach, we ate lunch. We finished both the sandwiches, all the leftover candy, and most of the fruit. We took turns trying to throw popcorn into each other's mouths, but an aggressive seagull quickly interrupted that game.

It screeched at me and, simultaneously, Mason and I screeched back.

Then we looked at each other and burst into hysterical laughter.

I packed everything, making sure I didn't forget any garbage. "Not too bad for a surprise lunch, was it?"

"Not bad at all," Mason said. "And I hope you know you're not the only one with surprises."

I raised my eyebrows. "What?"

"Check the outside pocket."

I pulled out our phones, which were in the waterproof pouch on the outside of the cooler. There was something else inside and I pulled it out, too. A portable speaker.

Mason casually plucked it from my hand. He rested it on Sparkles and pointed it towards us. "I've been putting a little playlist together."

"You have, have you?"

"Check this out." He turned on the first song.

It was a country song.

"Is this—"

"The first song we danced to," Mason said, grinning. "Thought I'd bring it back out so I can show you how much better I've gotten. I probably won't even step on your toes too many times."

I laughed. "Probably?"

His grin widened. "I'm not making any promises. Shall we?"

And so we danced.

Mason's playlist was a mix of two-step and jive. I didn't know how he'd done it, but almost every song on his playlist was one we'd danced to when I was teaching him. When I prodded him about this point, he told me he had an excellent memory for things that were important. It was a quarterback thing.

He spun me, I spun him. Sand flew as we danced and jumped and jived across our own private beach, careful to avoid the seashells. We danced under sun and shade. Sometimes, we took breaks to snack on fruit. Sometimes I danced by myself, showing him footwork and advanced concepts.

Mason didn't dance by himself. Instead, when I was taking a break, he lured Sparkles off the hammock and danced with the inflatable unicorn that was easily twice his size. It was the most ridiculous thing I had ever seen. Mason constantly apologized for stepping on Sparkles' toes. Then, he threw Sparkles up in the air and caught him, complete with a dramatic bow.

He was in the middle of his second dance with Sparkles — I was laughing so hard I was crying — when the song cut out and his phone rang.

Mason jogged over and answered. He had a quick conversation, then glanced at me with a smile that was slightly sad. "Tyler," he said. "Looks like you gotta get back home."

The bubble of our perfect day had popped.

I wasn't ready for it to end.

As if he could read my mind, Mason extended his hand. He winked. "But how about we have one more dance, first?"

ZOE

*M*ason stayed on my mind for the rest of the day. He was on my mind while I chewed through a burnt chicken thigh during family dinner, and he was still on my mind while I hunched over my desk and worked on a Physics problem. When my head hit my pillow, he was the last thing I thought about before falling asleep. And when I dreamed, I saw him and I dancing across clouds that were as soft as cotton candy.

Come Monday morning, not a single thing had pushed Mason McClellan out of my mind.

Nina found me in the hallway, grinning like a fool. She looped her arm through mine. "You need to tell me EVERYTHING."

And so I did. I told her about our impromptu sleepover. I told her about how we had breakfast together the next morning, just me and him walking in the surf. And I told her about our secret cove, the private beach where we danced. I didn't tell her I couldn't get Mason off my mind. I left that part out. I even tried to keep the excitement out of my voice, but I wasn't sure how much I succeeded.

Nina gawked. "That sounds amazing. Quick question for you — do you even remember Kevin?"

"Of course I remember Kevin," I said. That was technically true. I remembered Kevin. But when was the last time he popped in my head at random? Normally, thinking about him gave me butterflies, and caused my imagination to take off and wonder what a future between the two of us would look like. But now, it was almost like he was just another boy. A regular boy. Not that I was ready to admit that to anyone — including myself. "I still like Kevin. Besides, this whole thing with Mason — "

The words stopped my throat.

At the far end of the campus, Mason was casually leaning against a locker, one leg up, his arms crossed. He wasn't alone. Meredith stood beside him, her fingers twisting through her fair curls. She was smiling, laughing, and batting her eyelashes at him like she was a cartoon deer.

"Someone got all dressed up," Nina said, stopping beside me.

She was right. Meredith was wearing a short eyelet sundress with delicate spaghetti straps. A fine, gold chain necklace gleamed at her throat, and in her wedge-heeled sandals, she was almost at eye level with Mason. She looked like she should've been on a first date at a fancy restaurant, instead of heading to dance class.

The worst part?

It looked like her fancy clothes were working on Mason. He couldn't keep his eyes off her.

Not that I cared. Though I couldn't help glancing down at my blue and white striped shirt, white jean shorts and flip-flops. Stupid childish clothes that only emphasized how ordinary I was.

"You okay?" Nina asked.

"Why wouldn't I be?" I replied. I tried to keep my voice

firm and calm. But it was nearly impossible to ignore the sinking feeling in my chest. Or the pang of jealousy twisting through my stomach. "He's allowed to talk to her. He's supposed to talk to her. This whole thing we're doing, it's just a business transaction. The end goal is for him to end up with her."

Nina looked uncertain. "If you're sure…"

I nodded. "Let's go to class."

Nina started walking in the direction of Mason and Meredith. And why wouldn't she? That was the fastest way to class.

I grabbed her arm. "Let's take the scenic route."

Nina blinked, but said nothing.

We turned and walked in the other direction. I resisted the urge to look over my shoulder and watch Mason and Meredith flirt. It was none of my business, I reminded myself. I should be happy for his success.

"Zoe." Mason's voice carried through the open air.

I pretended not to hear him.

"Zoe, wait up."

I smiled weakly at Nina. "I'll catch up with you."

She glanced at Mason, then to me. "Are you sure?"

I nodded.

She waved, then marched towards class.

I put on my most cheerful smile. "Look at you go."

Mason immediately looked away, and scratched the back of his neck, clearly uncomfortable. "You mean Meredith? That was just nothing."

It didn't look like nothing. I folded my arms across my chest. "So, what's up?"

"I was wondering…"

Wondering what? How the rest of my weekend was? What I had for breakfast? If my heart had sunk all the way to my feet when I saw him with Meredith, or if it still had further to go? "Yes?"

He smiled shyly. "You know how to waltz?"

It turned out my heart could sink further. "I can teach you."

"You're the best," Mason said. "I've got to run. See you in Life Skills?"

His words echoed in my mind. I was the best? Clearly that wasn't true. I wasn't tall or gorgeous like Meredith. I wasn't the gold medal. Heck, I wasn't even the silver medal. To Mason, a girl like me was probably just a participation ribbon.

ZOE

I spent the next two days burying myself in dance and, unfortunately, Physics homework. Mr. Hinshaw called this week avalanche week — as in, an avalanche of assignments and quizzes were due. He claimed that this was the only way to prepare us for the real world — to make us as stressed and overworked as possible. I welcomed the homework. It was better to focus on Physics problems than it was to focus on Mason.

But, come Wednesday night, I was out of excuses. The football team had a rare night off, so I booked the dance studio for us after school.

I was midway through practicing my footwork when the door swung open.

Mason entered, wearing athletic shorts and a Rams jersey. His hair was messy, almost like someone had been running their fingers through it.

And who would've been doing that? I pushed the question from my mind. I knew he had an unconscious habit of messing with his hair. He'd been doing it since he was a kid.

It was almost a nervous tick — there was definitely no need for jealousy. Still, I decided it would be better for both me and Mason if I tried to keep a little professional distance between us. "Ready to waltz?"

"I'm all yours," Mason said.

I flushed. If only that were true. "The basic step is called the box step. When you do the box step, you'll create — surprise — a box on the floor. Start by putting your arm around me — your fingers should reach the small of my back."

Mason did. He smelled clean, like soap.

I looked into his eyes, and my breath hitched.

Keeping things professional was going to be harder than I anticipated. And it only got harder the more we danced. As I danced him through the motions — a forward half box, a backward half box, one two three, one two three — we fell into our familiar rapport.

But the entire time we danced, one fact plagued my mind. I wasn't teaching him to dance for me. I was teaching him to dance for Meredith. The longer we danced, the closer that fact came to the surface, until eventually, I could no longer hold it back.

"I'm surprised Meredith wants to learn the waltz," I said. "They rarely have a waltz at the Homecoming Dance Competition."

"Why not?"

"Not as exciting to watch as jive or swing," I said. "It's smooth and elegant, which translates to boring for the average high schooler."

Mason frowned in concentration, stealing a glance at his footwork as we waltzed through the empty room. "Meredith says we should be prepared for anything."

The idea of him dancing with Meredith at Homecoming

stung like a wasp bite. I raised my eyebrows. "So, it's official?"

"Not yet," Mason said. "I haven't asked her."

"But you want to go with her?"

Mason accidentally stepped on my toe.

I stumbled, tripped, and almost fell.

MASON

I caught Zoe before she hit the floor. It was clumsy and awkward, but at least she didn't hit her head and give herself a concussion.

"I'm so sorry. I wasn't paying attention to my feet."

But that wasn't entirely true. Honestly, it was her question that made me stumble. I'd wanted to go to Homecoming with Meredith for so long, I hadn't even considered whether it was still what I wanted. I just assumed it was. Who I really wanted to go with was—

No. That wasn't right. I mean, that would never work. She was my best friend's little sister, and, more importantly, she preferred smart guys. Guys who played chess and board games and were going to Harvard.

I steered her back into the rhythm of the waltz. "How're things going with Kevin?"

"Good enough." Zoe bent her elbow and put her hand on my shoulder. She was an elegant dancer, every move precise. "We see each other in the hallways. And now, he actually talks to me, too."

"And how do you feel about that?" Ugh. Chalk that question up to the year I spent in forced therapy sessions after my parents' divorce.

"I'm happy to report that I no longer feel like throwing up on his shoes every time he talks to me," Zoe said.

I laughed. "Proud of you."

"You should be. Soon I might even have a — gasp — boyfriend."

I stumbled again. This time I wasn't able to catch Zoe, and she fell to the floor awkwardly, landing on her hip.

She clutched her hip and winced. "Is it that difficult to believe?"

I felt like I'd kicked a baby rabbit. My stomach sank, my chest hurt, and there was an annoying stinging in the corner of my eyes. "Sorry, Zoo," I said, kneeling beside her. "You're a great teacher, but I'm not much of a waltzer."

She grimaced. "Don't worry. If Meredith asks, I'll lie."

I helped her to her feet. "You don't have to."

"What are friends for?" She brushed herself off. "And since we're friends, maybe you can tell me what to do next with Kevin. I'm not even sure he wants to go to Homecoming. Or on a date. Or that he's interested. For all I know, he's just hoping I'll buy another board game from him so he can get some commission."

I wanted to tell her that if Kevin wasn't interested, then he was an idiot. Instead, I fell back into my old persona: Mason the Dating Coach. "That's where the next step of our plan comes in. You're going to throw a party."

Zoe's eyes bulged.

"A small party," I added quickly. "Then, at the party, we'll put you in a position where Kevin has to ask you on a date. How's that sound?"

Zoe smiled through the pain. "Sounds like a plan."

"Great," I said. "Talk to Ty. Figure out when your mom's gone next, and that's when we'll plan the party."

It's great.

Yeah, just great.

ZOE

*O*n the first weekend of October, my mom was leaving town for a work conference. It was perfect timing, and once Mason learned of this opportunity, party planning began. We collected decorations, planned snacks and drinks, and put together a guest list. Then, sooner than I expected, the night of the party arrived.

I was a bundle of nerves. I'd never thrown a party before — at least not one where the guest list was bigger than Nina, Callie, Kenzie and myself. It turned out that party planning was a lot like dating. There were a lot of invisible rules that you were expected to know. For example, even though you told people the party started at seven, you shouldn't expect to see anyone until nine. You also needed to section off the parts of your house that you didn't want people to use. You couldn't just tell them not to go upstairs, you had to block the stairs with a chair. Or a couch.

I was glad Mason and Tyler knew what they were doing, because I was way out of my depths.

Nina stood in my bedroom, adjusting her outfit in front of the full-length mirror. For once, she wasn't wearing one of her signature band t-shirts. I'd talked her into a black miniskirt and a silky bronze camisole, which looked amazing against her smooth brown skin. She scanned her outfit. "What did your mom say when you told her about the party?"

Guilt gnawed at me. When mom left on her overnight trip, she left explicit directions that we were not to have people over. Those instructions were more aimed at Tyler than me, but that made me even more guilty. Mom trusted me. And she didn't want to come back to see that the house had been destroyed.

I stood beside Nina and touched up my lip gloss. "Didn't tell her."

Nina blinked. "You didn't tell her?"

"Is that so weird?" I hated how defensive I sounded. "Lots of people don't tell their parents things."

"Yeah, but... It's you."

I sighed. "I tried to talk to her. But she didn't want to hear anything I had to say. It's like she thinks I'm still a little girl. Precious little Zoe. She stuck me in that box, and she's not going to let me out. And she's definitely not going to let me have parties. So, I figured, what she doesn't know won't hurt her."

"What did Tyler say?"

"You know Ty," I said. My brother was too relaxed to care much. His philosophy was to deal with things as they happened. No sweat. "This party will be fine, right?"

"Absolutely," Nina said, dragging an eyeliner pencil along her lash line. "Everything's going to be fine. Is Kevin coming?"

He was, but I wasn't sure how I felt about that. A month ago, if someone had told me Kevin was coming to my house, I would've been thrilled. Or throwing up. One or the other. But now I wasn't so sure. "He'll be here," I said. I pointed to the board game I'd strategically set out on my desk. "That's why I have that set up."

Nina grinned. "You set up a board game so you can invite him to your bedroom?"

Gross. The thought of being alone with Kevin in my bedroom made me feel off, sort of like I just sipped milk that was past its best by date. I tried to calm my stomach. It was probably just nerves.

Downstairs, the front door opened.

I checked the clock. It was only 6:30. "I'm not ready."

Nina examined my outfit. "What could you possibly have left to do?"

I glanced in the mirror. Nina had tamed my crazy hair with a curling wand. My face was fully made up. And I was wearing a cute emerald green romper.

I knew I cleaned up well. But it didn't feel like enough, somehow.

"Make myself look pretty," I said.

"You're always pretty."

I smiled. "Takes one to know one."

Voices rose from the first floor. It wasn't our guests, it was just Tyler and Mason.

Nina mimed wiping the sweat from her forehead. "Don't worry, it's just Mason. We're safe."

But now that Mason was here, I felt more nervous than ever.

MASON

"So, dude, you invite Meredith to Homecoming yet?" Tyler asked as he grabbed us each a bottle of soda from the fridge. He handed me a root beer.

I took the root beer, twisted off the cap, and took a drink. The question Tyler asked had been at the top of everyone's minds lately. It seemed like no matter who I talked to — guys on the team, friends in class, even teachers — the subject turned to Homecoming. And when the subject turned to Homecoming, the conversation turned to Meredith. "There's no ink on that contract yet," I said, being purposefully vague.

"Better hurry up, before that ship sails." Ty raised his eyebrows. Parker had accepted his invitation to Homecoming last week, and he hadn't stopped preening like a peacock since.

Zoe and Nina entered the kitchen. Nina looked cute, sure, but my attention was immediately drawn to Zoe. She wore more makeup than usual, and her hair was curled, falling over her shoulders, but none of that mattered — she was beautiful with or without makeup. What really struck me was her eyes.

She'd always had pretty eyes, but tonight? They were beautiful.

She was wearing green, which made her eyes look a brighter, more vibrant emerald than ever. The startling color popped against her pale skin, and when our eyes met, something fluttered in my chest.

I glanced away and nervously ran my hand through my hair. She didn't catch me checking her out, did she? "Zoo," I said, while scrutinizing the label on my root beer. "We need to go over a game plan for you."

"Sounds good, Space Face," Zoe said. She tore open a party-size bag of salt and vinegar chips and poured them into a bowl.

She hadn't called me Space Face in a while.

While Nina and Tyler disappeared to put up the rest of the decorations, I helped Zoe stagger the snacks throughout the house.

"When the party starts, you need to position yourself near Kevin," I said. "So you two are alone, if you can."

"How am I supposed to do that without looking super awkward?"

"Magic," I said. I set a bowl of BBQ chips on the table in the basement. "Wait until he needs to get up to go do something. Like get food, or—"

"Go to the bathroom?" Zoe looked at me seriously. "I could corner him in there. Maybe knock on the door and tell him I'm waiting for him? Hey, Kev, after you're done peeing, would you mind asking me on a date?"

I laughed. "Maybe not the bathroom."

Zoe laid out a stack of napkins. "Okay. So after I get him alone, I…?"

"You know that restaurant you mentioned in Life Skills? The one where they let you break the plates after you're finished eating?"

"Snack N' Smash," Zoe said. She raised an eyebrow. "Good memory."

"It's a quarterback thing," I replied. "When you're alone with Kevin, bring up Snack N' Smash. Talk about how cool it is and how much you want to go. As long as he's not a complete idiot, he'll pick up on it."

"What if he doesn't?"

"He will," I said.

"Okay." Zoe scanned the room. "It looks good. Thank you."

The doorbell rang.

She looked mildly alarmed. "I thought people weren't supposed to get here until two hours after the party's meant to start?"

"They're not," I said. Then I shrugged. "Sometimes people don't follow the rules."

Zoe bit her lower lip. "Well. I guess I'm doing it. I'm off to play hostess. I can't believe you talked me into throwing a party. So unlike me. So unlike…"

She continued to ramble as she walked to the door, her voice fading.

One part of me was excited for her. This was it, her big party, her chance to get Kevin alone. Her chance to get a date with the smart guy she had a crush on. I was happy I could help.

But the other, bigger, part of me?

Indescribably jealous.

33

ZOE

*M*usic blasted through the living room stereo system and people milled around the ground floor of our house, laughing, dancing, playing games and digging into the snacks.

It was a success! About twenty-five people were here in total. Some I knew, some I didn't. Most people were clustered in the same cliques that they hung out with at school. I spotted Kenzie and Nina in the hallway, talking alone. Callie was with her friend Jace and his surfer buddies, who were all spread eagled outside on the patio furniture, playing a fast-paced card game that involved a lot of yelling. Tyler was sitting on the living room couch, surrounded by his football buddies. Parker was on his lap. Mason, sitting next to them, seemed to be constantly fighting off female attention himself. Too bad for him that Meredith wasn't here.

As for me, I spent the party split between two tasks: trying to find time alone with Kevin, and trying to make sure no one destroyed my house. Surprisingly, the first task was more difficult than the second. While at least one pop was spilled and a bowl of chips was overturned, there were no broken windows, stolen electronics, or couches set on fire. However, I didn't spot my first opportunity to be alone with Kevin until the party was nearing midnight.

There were about ten of us in the living room when Kevin excused himself to grab a drink from the kitchen.

My time had finally come. I exchanged a quick glance with Mason, and he gave me the smallest of nods. I then downed my entire bottle of soda so I'd have a convenient excuse. I set the empty bottle on a side table and followed Kevin into the kitchen.

He crouched by the fridge and examined his choices.

Now that I was alone with him, all the nervousness I'd successfully subdued came roaring back. My stomach gurgled, whether from nervousness or the soda I'd just finished, I didn't know. I shuffled across the floor. "Would you mind grabbing me one?"

"Sure." Kevin grabbed a soda, seemingly at random, and handed it to me.

Guzzling Grape. My least favorite flavor. But that was my fault — I didn't tell Kevin what kind I wanted, and obviously I couldn't expect him to read my mind. I twisted the cap off, took a drink, and tried to avoid grimacing. "Thanks for coming."

Kevin opened a Guzzling Grape soda for himself. "Yeah. I was supposed to be at a chess tournament tonight. It's kind of a league thing. But I thought that maybe this would be more fun. Plus, I wasn't lined up to play anyone that good this week."

"A party? More fun than chess? Impossible," I said, hoping that my sarcasm would be obvious.

It wasn't.

Kevin frowned.

Ugh. Stupid, stupid Zoe. When you made fun of the things someone liked, you were basically making fun of them, too. He probably felt like I'd come to the kitchen just to insult him. I needed to save face. Fast. "Thanks for picking out The Quest for El Dorado. I've been playing it a bit. It's a lot of fun."

Kevin's eyes lit up, and he smiled. The edges of his teeth were slightly purple from the grape soda. "You're enjoying it, then? That's excellent. I've read a lot about it on the forums, but I haven't tried it out myself. The components seem like they're really high quality. Did they provide you with card sleeves?"

"Uh, maybe?" I said. "I set it up in my room if you want to come look."

34

MASON

*W*hat were they doing in the kitchen, and why was it taking so long? I subtly — at least I thought it was subtle — positioned myself at the edge of the crowd, close to the kitchen. I was trying to eavesdrop so I could give Zoe tips for later. At least, that was the excuse I gave myself so I didn't feel like a spy.

Unfortunately, I couldn't hear anything they were saying over the laughter in the living room. We were a few hours into the party, and the groups of partygoers were well and truly mingling. Parker had disappeared, and now Tyler mimed playing a trombone while Nina laughed.. Zoe's friend Callie was chatting with Jace Griffin about the best places to surf in Beachbreak, and some other stuff. Honestly, their conversation was the hardest to pay attention to. They'd known each other forever, so the entire conversation felt like one big inside joke.

Kind of like the way it felt when I talked to Zoe.

I took a half-step towards the kitchen, hoping I'd be able to catch a snippet of their conversation.

Zoe exited the kitchen. She was drinking a grape soda —

her least favorite flavor — and smiling. Kevin followed close behind, and together, the two of them went upstairs.

I frowned. Why would they be going upstairs? The only thing upstairs was —

My stomach sank.

The only thing upstairs was Zoe's bedroom.

I squeezed the neck of my soda bottle so hard I thought it would shatter. My chest hurt and something curdled in my throat. I needed to relax. Relax. Don't worry about what's going on upstairs in Zoe's bedroom. It's probably nothing. I was probably reading too much into it. There were plenty of reasons you could invite a guy up to your bedroom at a party.

I took another sip of soda without tasting anything.

It was okay.

Everything was okay.

ZOE

*K*evin perched near the board game. He had a collection of pieces in his hand, and one by one, he was turning them over and examining them against the light. "These have a good weight to them," Kevin said. "A really nice feel. You should get the cards sleeved, though. When you play, what strategy are you using? I've read quite a bit of game theory. Do you go for the caves early and hope for a late push? Or try to get the early lead and block out the paths?"

Strategy? I hadn't given any thought to strategy. Then again, I'd only played against myself, and Tyler once. How much strategy could there be? Wasn't it just about moving pieces around the board and trying to get your adventurers to El Dorado? I didn't say my thoughts out loud because I didn't want to look stupid in front of Kevin. "I like to try new things," I said.

New things — like bluffing my way through a board game I had hardly played.

Kevin looked puzzled as he put the pieces back in the box. "I don't know why you would try something new," he said.

"Especially when there are people a lot smarter online coming up with strategies. Why not stick to what works?"

I didn't have an answer for that, so I changed the subject. "I've been too busy to read much lately. Lots of dance," I said.

He raised his eyebrows. "I didn't know you danced."

"Yep, on the team and everything," I said. How did he not know I danced? "Hey — have you heard about Snack N' Smash?"

Kevin slid the lid back on the board game box. "No, what is it?"

"It's this really cool restaurant where you get to eat, then break your plate after. I think it's Greek."

Kevin stared at me blankly.

Heat rose to my cheeks and a nervous energy entangled me. Mason said that Kevin would understand, that he'd pick up on my hint. That proved to be optimistic. Or worse — Kevin had picked up on my hint, but he wasn't interested. Was I an idiot for thinking this could work?

"You want to go?" I asked.

Ugh. I was doing it all wrong. He was supposed to ask me on the date, not the other way around.

"Like together?" Kevin asked.

"Yeah, sure, if you want. Like we totally could, but we definitely don't have to," I said. Nice save, Zoe. I clamped my lips together. At least if I stopped talking, I wouldn't make any more mistakes.

"We could go together," Kevin said. "It's a date."

The three words I've been waiting to hear my entire life: it's a date. With a boy. That I probably still had a crush on. I'd done it. I'd followed Mason's advice, and I had just planned my first date.

So why didn't I feel more excited about it?

If this was the moment I had spent the last year waiting for, why didn't I —

There was a loud bang as the front door slammed shut. The party went suspiciously quiet. Then, there was a loud shout. More of a roar, really.

I recognized the voice immediately.

Oh no.

Oh no no no.

I rushed out of my room and down the stairs and found —

My mom. Her face was red, her fists clenched. She slowly lifted her finger and pointed towards the door. "Get out. Everybody."

Slimy fingers of dread clasped my shoulders. My body went stiff and goosebumps pebbled my skin. I had broken the rules in my life only a handful of times, and this was by far the worst.

Mom's head turned towards me like a horror movie villain. "I explicitly said no parties."

"It wasn't a party," I said, coming down the stairs. "It was just a gathering." I knew exactly how pathetic I sounded.

Mom glanced at something behind me, and her eyes went wide.

What now? Was something broken? Was there a hole in the wall? I looked over my shoulder to see —

Kevin coming down the stairs.

It wasn't hard to guess what my mom was thinking. My face went white. "It's not what it looks like."

Mom pointed at Kevin. "Would you please leave? I need to speak with my daughter."

Kevin swallowed, nodded, and hurried out the door, leaving his jacket behind. Everyone else had already left. Except Tyler, who was pretending to be asleep on the couch.

"What were you thinking?" Mom asked.

"It's not like anything happened," I said.

"You're grounded."

I kept my mouth shut and nodded grimly. There was no arguing with mom. And in this case, what would my argument even be? That it was unfair that I wasn't allowed to have a party? Yeah, good luck with that one.

I trudged up the stairs and returned to my room. I finally got a date — a real date.

I just wasn't allowed to go on it.

36

ZOE

*B*eing grounded sucked for three reasons.

Reason number one: Kevin texted me to set up a time to go to Snack N' Smash, and I had to tell him I couldn't for the foreseeable future. I told him repeatedly that I wasn't trying to push him away, but, naturally, his texts were sent further and further apart. Not that they were ever super interesting. Still, a date was a date, and all things being equal, I actually wanted to, you know, go on it.

Reason number two: Tyler and I weren't allowed to do anything after school aside from dance for me and football for him. Everything else was explicitly forbidden. This meant no shopping on High Street with Nina and no strolls along the beach with Callie.

Reason number three: It was impossible to find time to teach Mason how to dance. Which meant that since the night of the party, I had literally no time alone with him, and he still hadn't learned all the dances Meredith wanted him to know. It was October now, and Homecoming was only a couple of weeks away.

On a bleary, overcast Friday where the ocean was the

same grey as the sky, Mason and I finally got an opportunity. Life Skills was cancelled because Mrs. Cortez was out sick. They couldn't find a substitute teacher, so every student got a free period. As luck would have it, one of the dance studios was empty.

Mason wandered through the empty studio. He paused in front of the floor-to-ceiling window, which looked out over the beach, and adjusted his tie. On game days, every player on the football team had to wear their game jersey over a collared shirt and tie. Mason said it was ridiculously uncomfortable, but I thought he looked extra cute in a nerdy, white-collar professional sort of way. Like a hot accountant. If those existed.

"This might be our last practice before Homecoming," I said, plugging my phone into the stereo. "And you only have one dance left to learn: salsa."

"If dancing salsa has anything in common with eating it, I should be a natural."

I groaned and rolled my eyes. "Ugh, dad joke alert."

Mason grinned. "More like hilarious joke alert."

"Whatever you say, Space Face," I said. "Stand beside me and watch my footwork."

He did.

"It's an eight count. Step forward, like this, then bring your feet together for a beat, then step back — kind of like a rock step — then back together again. If you can add a bit of wiggle with your hips, you're golden." I repeated the steps, this time exaggerating the wiggle in my hips.

He laughed. "All right. I'll shake my booty."

"That's not what I—"

Too late. Mason did the steps. As he did, he shook his butt in the most exaggerated fashion I'd ever seen. A professional dancer in a music video probably couldn't have matched his moves.

I looked away and shook my head, covering my grin with my hand. Despite his efforts to be ridiculous, it was clear how much better he'd gotten. And how used to spending time with him I'd gotten. Whenever we were alone together, time seemed to pass both exceptionally fast and not at all.

"Great booty shake," I said. "But your footwork is off. When you make your steps, you want to transition your weight. Right now, you're just tapping your feet."

"Tapping my feet with style," Mason corrected, adding a booty shake for emphasis.

"Yes, I suppose some would consider that style."

He pushed me playfully. "Okay, what next."

"Now we do it together." I skipped to the stereo and turned on the salsa playlist. "Ready?"

Mason bowed and extended his hand.

I took it.

He pulled me into him, so close I could smell the citrus in his aftershave.

The heady scent overwhelmed me for a moment. I briefly thought of biting his jawline, then immediately shoved that thought away. I didn't know a lot about boys but I strongly suspected that they didn't want random girls to bite their faces. I cleared my throat. "On three. Annnnnd three."

We danced together, and once again, time disappeared. Not only did Mason keep up with the rhythm, but he didn't step on my toes, either. Once I was satisfied with his foot-work — which didn't take long — I taught him a few more moves. Before I knew it, we were spinning, sweating, laughing, and wiggling our hips in perfect rhythm.

Time didn't start again until I heard a knock at the door.

Irrational anger boiled in my stomach. Who would interrupt us? The dance studio was free until next period, and we still had fifteen minutes left. I was about to open the door—

or to yell at the person to go away, I hadn't decided yet — when the door opened.

Meredith slipped inside, closing the door lightly behind her. She was wearing tight jeans that showed off her perfect figure, and a loose white tunic top. Her blonde hair was pulled in a side ponytail. If there was ever a natural beauty on this earth, it was Meredith. She eyed Mason and batted her eyelashes.

The boiling anger in my stomach was now steaming out my ears. I swallowed it down and tried to look as pleasant as possible. Meanwhile, Meredith the Interrupter was giving Mason her best doe-eyed look and smiling at him like they were already a thing. They weren't.

I was sure they weren't. I'd asked Ty.

Meredith closed her eyes and stepped to the music. On anyone else, the move would've looked ridiculously over the top. But for Meredith? It worked as though she was some kind of super sensual angel who'd descended from the heavens just to grace us with her presence.

She opened her eyes, a surprised expression on her face. Like she'd just lost herself in the music by accident. Like it wasn't a calculated move to make Mason look at her. "Would you mind if I cut in, Zoe? I hear you've been training my date for Homecoming, and I'd like to see if he's ready."

Her date? Ugh. I gritted my teeth. This was what I had agreed to. I plastered on a pleasant smile while grinding my molars into dust. "Absolutely, I don't mind at all."

Mason shot me a sideways glance. I stared back, trying to keep my face arranged in a grin. Then, he took Meredith's hand, and they danced around the room.

Stupid smile still plastered on my face, I stared at them. I hoped it would be awkward. I hoped he'd step on her toes, or that she'd fall and twist her ankle. Nothing serious — just enough to make her not want to go to Homecoming with him. Or maybe there could be an earthquake, a slight tremor that would knock them both off balance. As long as they didn't fall on top of each other.

But their dance was not awkward. It was smooth as cream. Meredith moved like a woman. So unlike me. Whenever I danced, I still felt like a kid trying to be an adult. But Meredith? She was an adult. She was mesmerizing. She probably smelled good, too, and I hated her for it. She danced so close to Mason that if they turned their heads, their lips would probably touch.

I wanted to rip out my hair and run screaming from the room. I was just about to head for the door when Meredith broke away.

I took a deep breath.

Meredith curled her finger under his tie, then straightened it out, smoothed his collar, and patted his shoulders. "Looks like I'll see you at Homecoming."

I thought I heard one of my teeth actually crack.

Meredith smiled at me. "And you! You must be an absolutely wonderful teacher. Look how good he's doing now. Thank you so much for teaching my date how to dance, but I can take him off your hands from here. I'll be sure to put in a word with Coach, though, you have all the makings of a future dance captain."

"Thanks," I said glumly.

Meredith waved, blew Mason a kiss, then pranced away, a deer through a meadow.

I didn't watch her leave, I only watched Mason's eyes follow her. His expression was impossible to read, but I was there for their dance. It didn't take a genius to see that guys like Mason went for girls like Meredith. They didn't go for girls like me.

Ugh. I had a feeling that dance was going to haunt me.

37

ZOE

*a*nd the dance did haunt me. In my nightmares. I dreamed they were dancing through all the amazing places Mason and I had danced. He and Meredith danced at the floating Night Market, in the dance studio, and on High Street. Worst of all, they danced at our Secret Cove. In this last part of the dream, I was trapped inside my floating unicorn, sitting on the hammock, and staring at them as they kissed on the beach.

I woke up angry at real Mason because of dream Mason's betrayal. I knew it was irrational, but I still had a sinking feeling in my gut. If Mason and Meredith got together, like officially together, would he take her to Secret Cove? Probably. It was a great place for a date.

But, ugh. It hurt. It felt inappropriate, a violation of a sacred space. And how stupid was it that I was annoyed at him for something that hadn't even happened yet — and might never happen?

For the better part of Saturday, I pushed those thoughts from my mind as I focused on my Physics homework. Mom and Ty bustled around the house, preparing for an overnight trip to UC Berkeley, which was Tyler's top pick. Just before they stepped out the door, Mom turned to me and rattled off a list of rules.

"No parties," Mom said.

I already knew that one. I smiled and nodded politely.

"No one is allowed to step foot inside the house, and you're not allowed to leave. You're still grounded. And I'll know if you leave."

Her threat was vague, but earlier in the afternoon she'd demanded that I turn over my phone. I did, mostly because I couldn't risk extending my grounding if I ever wanted to go on my date with Mason. Kevin. My date with Kevin. Why was I thinking about a date with Mason? The point was, her threat was vague, but I suspected she might've installed a tracking app on my phone. If I left the house, she'd know.

"And you'll answer my texts immediately," Mom said.

"Absolutely," I said.

She looked at me sternly. "All right. You can microwave a freezer meal."

Yum.

"Is there anything else you need before your brother and I leave?"

Yes, there was one thing I desperately wanted. I took a deep breath. "I know I'm grounded," I said.

Mom raised an eyebrow. "But?"

"But the Homecoming dance is next Saturday."

Mom sighed. "I'm not happy about the party, but I would never keep you two away from the Homecoming Dance. You'll just be under a strict curfew."

That solved problem one. Time for problem two. I smiled. "Thank you. Also…"

"Also what?" Mom's tone carried a warning.

"Also, I was asked on a date. And I'd like to be allowed to

go on it before he loses interest. And there'd be a curfew and everything," I said.

Tyler, who was standing by the door, snickered. "Bold move, dude."

I glared. I hated when he called me dude. But that was Ty. He called everyone dude. Even teachers.

Mom jangled her car keys and considered my ask. "Behave tonight. You don't leave the property, you don't throw any parties. You be good, and I'll let you go on your date."

My spirits lifted. "Deal."

Mom and Ty left, and I prepared myself for an evening by myself. I munched on popcorn as I went through next week's Physics assignments. I texted Nina, hoping to chat, but she didn't reply. Maybe she actually had plans on a Saturday night. After watching a few episodes of some new sitcom on Netflix, I turned off the TV and prepared for bed, despite the fact that it was only 7:30pm. If I was asleep, then there was no chance I could get in trouble.

I turned off my bedroom lights and snuggled beneath the duvet. My eyes slowly closed.

Something tapped against my window.

I rolled over, not bothering to look. The forecast had threatened rain for the past week. Maybe it was finally starting. I closed my eyes tighter.

Tink.

Tink.

Thunk.

That was like no rain storm I'd ever heard. I sat up and watched my window.

Something bounced against the glass. Tink.

Was someone throwing things?

I creeped over to the window and peeked out.

Mason stood in the middle of my backyard, holding a

handful of pebbles. He wore blue jeans, a collared shirt, and a blazer with a single button done up. He looked amazing, like a male model. Like he had taken great care to get ready tonight.

He looked like he was going on a date.

My nightmare rushed back. He must've already asked out Meredith. Maybe they were going on a date tonight, a date before Homecoming. Maybe he was going to take her to Secret Cove. I gritted my teeth and slid my window open. "Can I help you?"

"So formal," he said. "Are you in your pajamas? It's like seven."

"It's eight."

"That's basically seven."

It was not "basically" seven, and I was almost annoyed enough to correct him. I gestured to his fancy pants outfit. "Why are you wearing that?"

"For our date."

I was so shocked I almost fell out the window. "Our date?"

"Your practice date," Mason said. "Ty said your mom might let you go out with Kevin next week. I figured you'd want some practice so you could figure things out first."

It was a sweet gesture, but the sweetness only made it hurt more when I had to turn him down. "I can't," I said. "If I leave the house, Mom'll kill me. And then Kevin will be going on a date with a ghost."

Mason didn't just roll his eyes, he practically rolled his entire head. "Just trust me. Fifteen minutes, then I'm ringing your doorbell to pick you up for our date."

Before I could respond, he jogged off.

I watched him go, then closed my window. Trust him? Fifteen minutes? What was that all about? Didn't he under-stand that no matter how badly I wanted to go somewhere with him, I couldn't? At least not if I wanted to live long enough to graduate.

I closed the curtains and considered his words.

Just trust me.

I did trust him. He'd been so nice, so helpful. Didn't I owe it to him to trust him one more time?

Okay.

I could trust him one more time.

It was time to get ready, and I only had thirteen minutes left.

MASON

*F*ifteen minutes after tossing pebbles at Zoe's window, I stood on her front step, nervously shifting my weight from foot to foot. Mentally, I reviewed the dance steps she'd taught me. I wasn't taking her dancing, not tonight, but whenever I was nervous, I focused on the steps. I liked to think of it as extra practice.

Speaking of practice, I knew she'd feel better if she had a practice date under her belt. And what better way to start off a practice date than with a rose? It was the classic first date flower. But, as they say, presentation is everything. So just before I rang the doorbell, I put the rose stem between my teeth and exaggerated my cheesiest smile.

Footsteps came to the door.

My heart thudded in my chest.

The door opened.

And there was Zoe.

Her dark hair was pulled back off her face, making her green eyes look bigger and sparklier than ever. She wore a black silk dress that stunningly contrasted with her pale, creamy skin. She looked delicate, beautiful. Perfect.

My jaw dropped and the rose fell from my mouth. I yipped, juggled it, and caught the stem, pricking my middle finger on one thorn. I tried to turn my rose drop into something that looked intentionally cool, but I was pretty sure I failed.

Zoe laughed and plucked the rose from my hand. "How 'bout I take that before you throw it on the ground?"

I looked her in the eyes. "I always thought calling someone jaw-droppingly beautiful was just an expression, something that didn't actually happen. Then you opened the door."

Her cheeks went pink, and she smiled. "Thanks."

As quickly as her smile came, it faltered.

My heart faltered with it. "What's wrong?"

"I can't go on the date," she said. "I don't know if Ty told you, but I can't leave the property."

Now it was my turn to smile. "And that's the first lesson you need to learn on your practice date. If a guy is worth your time, he'll have a backup plan. Just follow me."

I offered her my hand.

39

ZOE

*M*y heart was in my throat. If I took Mason's hand, I would follow him anywhere. To High Street, to our Secret Cove. It didn't matter what the consequence was — I'd go with him. I needed to stay strong now, before it was too late. "I can't. I want to, but I can't."

Mason smiled warmly. "I'd never do anything to hurt you, Zoe."

I took his hand.

Mason didn't lead me towards the street. Instead, he led me around my house into my backyard. Soft music was coming from somewhere. I couldn't pick out the song. It was like something out of a restaurant.

Mason squeezed my hand and motioned to the treehouse. There was a soft glow emanating from the doorway. "Welcome to the Treehouse Café," Mason said. "It's the most exclusive restaurant in Beachbreak. It's so exclusive, there's only one table. Fortunately, I know the owner, so I was able to squeeze us in. Ladies first."

I smiled so hard my cheeks hurt. This couldn't be real. This couldn't actually be happening to me right now. Rung by rung, I climbed the ladder to the treehouse. I was secretly paranoid that I would slip off. That would be just like me — a boy plans something super nice, and I ruin it by plummeting off a tree and breaking my arm.

A red tablecloth was draped over the small table in the center of the treehouse. Flickering wax candles gave off a soft glow and made the treehouse warm as a blanket fresh out of the dryer.

It was difficult to breathe. I couldn't believe Mason had done this. How did he pull this off? I was at home all day. How was he able to sneak through the yard and into the treehouse to set everything up?

I took a seat. "This is incredible."

Mason nodded and sat opposite me. "Only the best. I trust the Treehouse Café is to your satisfaction?"

"So formal." I laughed. The Treehouse Café was amazing, and I didn't have the words to express it. "So what are we eating? Did you sneak some food in here, too?"

Mason reached under the table, pulled out a menu, and handed it to me.

"You're joking," I said, taking the laminated — yes, laminated — menu from his hands. Apparently, the Treehouse Café had several menu options available. Burgers and fries, four cheese lasagna, and a fancy surf and turf were all listed. For drinks, we had a variety of sodas. I tapped the menu. "I've noticed that there are no prices listed?"

"Already paid."

"And should I expect that when I'm on a date with a gentleman?"

"Depends on the gentleman," Mason said. "I've always thought that whoever asks, pays. But you can offer to split it. Sometimes people prefer that. When I ask a girl on a date, I always offer to pay. If she offers to split it, then we do that. Whatever makes everyone comfortable."

"Well, if you're paying, I'm going to have three surf and turfs, two burgers and fries, and—"

"We're definitely splitting it," Mason said, grinning.

I laughed. "Okay, okay. This might be really simple… but I want the burger and fries. And a cream soda. And… maybe a churro sundae for dessert?"

"Absolutely."

I stared at Mason, waiting for him to magically produce the entire meal. He was basically magic, after all. But the only thing he produced was his phone. He sent a text, then slid his phone back in his pocket.

"Normally, it's frowned upon to use your phone on a date," Mason said. "Avoid it if you can. This was an exception. Our food should be here in twenty minutes. Which is perfect — that'll give us enough time to practice the basics of going on a first date. Now, when you're on your first date, you'll probably feel nervous."

"I don't feel nervous right now," I said. It was true — I never felt nervous around Mason like I did with other guys. Instead, I felt comfortable. Being with Mason was like being curled up next to a roaring bonfire on a hot summer night, the kind of night you wanted to last forever.

"Because it's not a real date," Mason said. "But with Kevin, you'll probably be nervous while you're waiting for your food to arrive."

"Okay, let's assume I'm an awkward, nervous mess." I leaned forward. "What should I do to impress my date?"

Mason adjusted the candle in the center of the table so it was out of our eyeline. "First, you need to rethink your idea of what a date is. You don't want to go on a date thinking you need to impress some guy. And you don't want a guy going on a date thinking he needs to impress you."

"Why not?"

"Because if you're impressing somebody, or he's

153

impressing you, you're both just playing pretend. Worse, you're just pretending to be someone that you think the other person will like. The best-case scenario is that they do like you while you're playing pretend, which means they like who you're pretending to be, not who you really are."

This was the first time I had doubted Mason. I crossed my arms. "You're not going to give me some cheesy 'be yourself' message, are you?"

"I one hundred percent am," Mason said.

"So I should show up in a spaghetti stained sweatshirt and pajama pants, with an inch of grime in my hair because I haven't washed it in three days?"

"Why not? At least then they know what they're getting." Mason laughed. "But seriously, you want to be the best version of yourself, but you still want to be you. You want to be the effortlessly confident Zoo that jives at the Night Market or waltzes in Secret Cove. The thing is, the first date is just the first page of a book. You still got a whole story to tell after that. And in any story, you can only pretend something for so long. At some point it comes down to you, to him, and to chemistry."

I felt like I should take notes. "Okay, how do you get chemistry, Mr. Expert?"

Mason shrugged. "I wish I could tell you. Chemistry is the one thing you can't force. Sometimes it's there, sometimes it's not. Sometimes, a guy can check every box on your list, and there'll be no chemistry. Just nothing. And sometimes, you find chemistry with the people you know you shouldn't have chemistry with. The people you're not allowed to have chemistry with."

People like your brother's best friend, who was taking another girl to Homecoming. People like that.

"Knock knock!" Nina's shout came from the backyard. A moment later, her face appeared in the door of the treehouse.

She was wearing another band shirt. She was also wearing a clip-on bowtie. She climbed into the treehouse and set a big bag of food on the table. "Madam. Monsieur. Your order is served."

I clapped my hands delightedly and rocked back in my chair. I almost rocked back too far and tipped over, but thankfully, I caught myself on the edge of the table. "You've been avoiding me all day, and now you're here?"

"Mason's orders." Nina grinned and unpacked the food. "The front door was open, so I left the churro sundaes in the freezer. If there's anything else you need... well I can't help you, I have a concert to go to, but I'm sure you'll figure it out. Enjoy!"

Nina left.

I was nearly at a loss for words. "How did you..."

"Pull this off?" Mason asked. He pulled two china plates out of the bag, set them on the table, then unpacked the rest of our food. "Sometimes, the play breaks down and you have to scramble to make something out of nothing. Sometimes, you have a practice date planned, and people get grounded. So you improvise. But, why don't we put the dating lessons on hold and focus on what's important? The food."

I dug into my burger and fries. Mason got the same. When I asked him what he would've done if I ordered the lasagna or the surf and turf, he told me that he had already scoped out the full menus at each of the restaurants and had a plan prepared for each one. He told me that a good quarterback always has a plan — even when things looked like they wouldn't work out. Between bursts of laughter, we finished our food.

"Since you aced the dinner portion of your date — meaning you didn't spill on yourself — "

"Wait, I was being judged for that?"

He winked. "Only a little. Don't worry, you'll never top

this one date I went on. The girl straight up shot hummus out of her nose."

I grimaced.

"That's the face I made too," Mason said. He quickly cleaned the plates with a napkin, then exited the treehouse. "Come on."

My curiosity was killing me. What could he possibly have planned next? I followed him down the ladder and out to the driveway.

Mason handed me a plate. "You're going to Snack N' Smash, which means that at the end of your date, you'll each get to smash your plate. I figured that since you're not an all-star quarterback — like some people I know — you'd want a practice throw."

I held the plate tentatively. "You want me to break it?"

"Don't worry — it's only a practice plate."

"What about the shards?"

"I brought a broom with me."

"If you say so." I raised the plate, but hesitated. It was weird to think that I was deliberately going to break something. It went against every instinct I had. I looked at Mason one more time for reassurance, and when he nodded, I threw the plate against the concrete.

It shattered into six pieces.

A thrill ran through me. "How'd I do?"

"Almost perfect. But I think I should show you how it's done. Properly."

I laughed and crossed my arms. "All right, Space Face. Let's see how an all-star quarterback throws a plate."

Mason held the plate like a football, his expression serious. He pump faked once. Twice. Then he nodded to me, drew his arm back to throw the plate—

And it slipped out of his hand and fell behind him.

CRACK. It split in half.

And so did my sides. I was laughing so hard that I almost collapsed to my knees before remembering that there were broken pieces of glass on the driveway. Gasping for air, I wandered to the side yard and fell in the cool grass.

Mason glared at the plate like it had betrayed him, then scratched his head, looking remarkably like a confused monkey from the zoo. "Maybe you should be the one giving me tips."

I recovered enough breath to reply. "Definitely. Do you want any help cleaning?"

"After I drop you off," Mason said.

I hooked my arm through his, and he walked me to the front door.

"If you're dating the right sort of gentleman, he'll walk you to your door," Mason said. "Or at least he'll make sure you got inside okay. But that's just being polite."

I put my hands in his and looked at him. He was handsome enough to break hearts. "What now?" I asked. "We tell each other how lovely the night was?"

"Exactly," he said. "And sometimes this is where the first kiss happens."

Heat rose to my cheeks. "Right. That."

Our eyes met, and a spark of electricity shot through me, making my skin tingle. Mason held my gaze for a long moment, before looking away. "Are you ready for your first date? And your first kiss?"

"Thanks to you," I said. Instinctively, I wrapped my arms around him, pulling him into a hug and resting my head on his chest. "Thank you. For everything. I just hope Kevin can live up to the example you set."

"I'm sure he can," Mason replied, squeezing me tight. "He's much smarter than me."

I kept my arms around him, my head on his chest, listening to his heartbeat. I never wanted the hug to end.

157

Next Friday, I'd have my date with Kevin. Then on Saturday, Mason would have his Homecoming date with Meredith. It was all happening too soon. It felt like as soon as I let him go, it would be Homecoming.

And I wasn't ready for that.

40

MASON

$\mathcal{T}$here was only one word I could use to describe Homecoming Week at Beachbreak: insane. There were so many pep rallies and parades that they became one big blur of fight songs, cheerleaders, and roaring students. Everywhere I went, people were asking me about our Homecoming game against the Santa Mara Tide. Students, teachers, alumni. They all wanted me to personally guarantee a victory against our biggest rival.

Coach even pulled me out of Life Skills class for the week so I could spend the period reviewing game tape. This meant that I didn't get to see Zoe for most of the week.

As the week went on, the forecast got worse and worse, and by the time Friday Night Lights rolled around, the rain fell in sheets and drowned out the roar of the crowd.

The clock was counting down to zero all too quickly.

I scrambled out of the pocket, my cleats struggling to grip the mud.

A giant with black lines painted under his eyes chased me. I checked the clock — only three seconds left, and we

159

were down by four points. I dug my feet into the ground and lofted the ball.

CRUNCH.

The giant leveled me, wrapping his arms around me, tackling me and driving his shoulder into my chest as we fell.

Air left my body.

Our side of the crowd groaned.

I swore. The pass must've been incomplete. There would be no time left on the clock, and we'd lose to our biggest rival. Not how I wanted Homecoming to go.

"You lose, sucker," the giant said. Still on top of me, he grabbed a handful of mud and discretely flicked it in my helmet.

The grime clung to my mouth guard, and I tasted mud and dirt.

I also saw red.

I shoved the guy off of me and leaped to my feet. I was about to go after him when Tyler grabbed my shoulder pads. He pushed me away and pointed to a flag lying in the mud. "Roughing the passer," he said. "We get another play."

Another play.

One more shot.

The giant swore at the ref, then he looked at me and wiggled his fingers. "I'm coming for you, Seven."

I wiped the mud from my eyes and walked back to the huddle. "All right, boys. We got one more shot at this. So let's send these hopped up idiots home crying," I said. "Deuce Left Mesh. Bryan, on the cross, break deep and pull the safety. He doesn't go with you, I'll hit you. He does, I'll hit Tyler on the backside go. Ready? Break."

We set up at the line of scrimmage.

The giant stood up and pointed out our formation. "Watch the crossing routes, Seven's going to hit them on the crossing routes. Just like we saw on tape."

I chuckled and met his eyes. "You've been watching our tape, man?"

He glared at me. "Yeah."

I winked. "Then watch this."

I snapped the ball.

The defense crashed the line of scrimmage and the giant broke through. He tore after me, his teeth gritted together, murder in his eyes. He opened his arms to swallow me whole—

And I ducked beneath him.

Aimed for my receiver.

Threw.

The ball stayed in the air forever. I swore I could see rain drops spinning off of it as it spiraled to the end zone.

Bryan blew past his defender, leaped in the air, and caught the ball.

Touchdown.

Game over.

The crowd erupted in deafening cheers and screams.

I pumped my fist and shouted until my voice was hoarse.

I wasn't proud — I definitely looked over my shoulder at the giant in the mud and watched his anger turn to sadness. Then, I was off down the field, running beside Tyler, trying to find Bryan in the midst of the crowd storming the field.

Tyler smacked my helmet and held out a fake mic. "Mason McClellan, you've just won the Homecoming game, you're going to the dance with the hottest girl in school, and you even got my sister a date with the nerd of her dreams, how do you feel?"

All the excitement I'd been feeling drained from my body, replaced by a pang of jealousy. Other than winning the Homecoming game, I wasn't sure how I felt about any of that. But I had to remember — Zoe wasn't here. It was her date tonight. She wanted the nerd. Kevin was her type.

"I feel great," I lied. "And I bet if we hurry, we can see the two nerds off on their date."

I still had something I wanted to give her.

41

ZOE

I turned off the radio and sat in the silence of my bedroom. I wished I could have been at the football game. I wanted to be in the stands, clapping, screaming, cheering on Mason, Tyler, and the rest of the team. But I was at home, getting ready for my first date.

Nina poked my side. "You're zoning out again."

"Sorry," I said.

Nina gestured to the outfits lying on my bed. "Do we have a winner?"

My choices were limited. My black dress was the fanciest, but I'd worn that on my practice date with Mason. I wanted to keep that memory special. Between Mason and I. My eyes moved disinterestedly between my other options — a red fit and flare dress with a scalloped hem and a boring beige shirtdress with distinct secretary vibes.

Honestly, I wanted to stay at home in my pajamas and watch Netflix. But Nina wouldn't let that happen, so I grabbed the shirtdress.

She raised her eyebrows. "Okay, so I laid that out as a joke… are you feeling okay?"

"Fine," I said quickly. I set down the shirtdress and grabbed the red one instead.

"Really?"

My stomach turned. I hadn't eaten much today. I told myself I was just saving room for Snack N' Smash, but there was only so long you could lie to yourself. Secretly, I was dreading my date. It felt all wrong. Why was I going through with this, again?

Nina hugged me. "You'll be great. You have nothing to be nervous about. It's only a date with Kevin. It's not like you're going out with Mason or something."

"Weird thing to say," I muttered, stepping into the red dress. "Zip me?"

Nina gave it a nod of approval, and I spun around so she could zip me up. "Is it really a weird thing to say? You two have been spending a lot of time together. Like a lot. And you're seriously trying to tell me that there's nothing there?"

"I already told you — he's just being nice," I said. I wanted — desperately — for there to be something between me and Mason. The last few weeks I'd spent teaching him to dance and learning how to date had been some of the most fun in my life. But just because I desperately wanted there to be chemistry, didn't mean there was actually chemistry. Plus, there was the whole Meredith thing to contend with. "He's going to Homecoming with Meredith. If he wanted to go with me, he would've asked. He's that type of guy."

Nina looked doubtful, but she said nothing.

I examined myself in the mirror. I looked... average. And average would never cut it with a guy like Mason. He wanted the best — he deserved the best. And that was Meredith. Not me.

MASON

*T*here wasn't a thing in the world that made me more nervous than giving someone a present. Especially someone I cared about.

I sat on a couch in the living room of Zoe's house, the bag on my lap. It felt strangely heavy, as though it carried a weight I couldn't see. Maybe that was the problem. After all this time, I wasn't sure whether the gift was appropriate. Was this a "just friends" gift, or was it trying to be something more?

Maybe I shouldn't give it to her. If anyone asked, I could just pretend that I brought a spare change of clothes for after the football game.

"Zoe, you ready yet?" Tyler called, sitting on the couch beside me. He was antsy to get to the team's afterparty.

A door creaked open, and a moment later, Nina appeared at the top of the stairs. "She's coming," Nina said. She jogged down the stairs, kneeled, and pulled out her phone to take a picture. She paused. "Are we the embarrassing parents in this situation?"

The couch groaned as Tyler stood. He wandered across

the room until he was beside Nina. "Mom's not here. Someone needs to embarrass her. And to capture this moment for the world to see. My little sister, on her first date with a nerd."

"First date, period," Nina corrected.

I got off the couch and stood behind the two of them. I took a deep breath and looked to the top of the stairs.

Zoe was there. She was wearing a red dress that made her look like something out of a fairytale. Her dark hair tumbled down her back, and her cheeks were bright pink — she was blushing from the attention. I loved it when she blushed.

How many times was she going to make my jaw drop? As far as I was concerned, Zoe was the most beautiful girl on the planet. She was a sunset over an ocean, the alpenglow of the mountains, and the stars on a moonless night — all at once. My gift bag almost slipped out of my hand, and I had to make a conscious effort to hold on to it. I wanted to give her the present, but I didn't want to do it in front of Nina and Tyler.

Ty nodded approvingly. "Dude, you clean up nice."

"Nothing a girl loves more than being called dude," Nina said, rolling her eyes. She smiled at Zoe. "You, my friend, look absolutely incredible."

"Thank you," Zoe said, her voice quiet. Our eyes met.

Still struggling to find the right words to compliment her, I opened my mouth to say something—

But the doorbell rang.

Tyler darted to the doorway too fast and swung it open.

"I'm here to pick up Zoe?" Kevin's voice was nails on a chalkboard.

Tyler let him inside. He looped his arm casually around Kevin's shoulder. "Now, if you're taking my little sister on a date, there're some rules you're going to need to follow, my dude. The first rule is—"

"The first rule is that you're not supposed to listen to Tyler," Nina said. She dug her claws into Tyler's wrist and practically dragged him out of the room. "I don't know how anyone puts up with you. Why don't you just…"

Nina's voice was lost as she and Ty disappeared into another area of the house, leaving me, Kevin, and Zoe alone.

Kevin didn't even bother to look at me. Apparently, dumb jocks were beneath him. "We need to go," he said. "The clock is ticking on my ride share. You ready?"

The clock is ticking? Was he kidding? With the amount of effort that Zoe put into her appearance, and the way she looked, that was something to be savored. Not rushed. Why would you rush through something that beautiful? That was like sitting on the beach and yelling at the sun to hurry up and set, already.

"Oh, ok," Zoe said. "Sorry. I'll catch up in just a sec."

"Don't take too long." Kevin scurried out of the house.

It was just me and Zoe.

I could barely breathe. If there was ever a time to give her the present, this was it. I needed to do it. I needed to do it now. So why did the bag weigh so much? Why was it so hard to just hand it over? I couldn't believe this was happening. Was I really just going to let Zoe walk away and go on a date with that jerk?

My lips parted. I had to say something, anything, but no words came out. What could I say that would sum up the best weeks of my life?

Zoe took a step towards me.

My breath caught.

She hugged me and rested her head on my chest.

I wrapped my arms around her and squeezed. Sometimes, when you hug a person, it just feels right. Like you're connected with each other. And that's how I felt when I hugged Zoe. When I danced with Zoe. When I laughed with

Zoe. It was right. I wanted — desperately — to tell her how I felt, but it was too late to stop what was happening. Wasn't it?

"Thank you," she said. "For everything."

"Of course," I replied, squeezing her tightly. "I'm always around if you need me."

She pulled away from me. "I hope that's true."

I forced a smile to hide the cracks in my heart. "Always."

She stood on her tiptoes, kissed my cheek, then turned to the door.

Instinctively, my fingers rose to where her lips had been. I wanted to say something. Needed to say something. To at least give her the present. But how would I do that without messing up her date? Or completely ruining it. She wanted Kevin, I reminded myself. Kevin. Not Mason. I stood by the front door and watched her leave.

Kevin met her halfway down the driveway, and the two of them linked arms and walked towards the car.

There was no misery worse than watching the person you love walk away with someone else.

Kevin opened the door. Zoe got in the backseat and looked at me through the window. There was something in her eyes, something sad.

No, there wasn't. There couldn't be. I was wrong, I was just seeing what I wanted to see.

Kevin got in the car, the brake lights flared, and the car pulled away from the curb just as the first few drops of rain were falling again. The smell of fresh rain surrounded me.

I suddenly felt exhausted, and ancient. It was like every hit I'd taken during the Homecoming football game all piled on me at once. Somehow, I felt every bump, every bruise, every cut. I felt my ankle twist as cleats stepped on the back of my leg, my shoulder pop when the giant landed on me, my

IT HAD TO BE MASON

head ring after diving for a first down. I had to lean against the doorframe to keep from crumpling.

"Dude, you ready to celebrate?" Tyler was standing behind me.

"I'm tired, man. I'm going to head home."

Tyler looked at me skeptically. "You okay?"

"Think the hits are catching up with me." I gave him a fist bump. "Good game, man."

"Good game."

I stepped out into the rain, and Tyler shut the door.

I was still holding the gift bag. I peeked inside and smiled sadly. Zoe deserved this present. After all the work she put in, she definitely deserved it. And it was important to support the people you cared about, even if they were moving away from you. But I couldn't go back inside and put it in the house. I'd have to leave it for her somewhere else.

Somewhere only she would find it.

43

ZOE

*O*ur car drove through the rain, the tires splashing through puddles that reflected the neon lights of High Street. Kevin didn't talk much during the drive, choosing instead to pull out his phone and play a game of chess online. That was okay. I didn't feel like talking. If we talked, I didn't know what I would say.

By the time we reached Snack N' Smash, the rain was coming down hard.

Kevin nervously stared out the window. "Do you think it'll stop?"

"Doubt it," I said.

He frowned. "We'll have to run for it."

"Looks like it."

Kevin nodded, steeling himself, then opened the door and sprinted to the restaurant, covering his head. He'd left me alone in the car.

I leaned across the backseat and closed the door. Mason wouldn't have left me alone. Mason would've brought an umbrella. Or given me his jacket as a shield. Or something. He'd improvise. Treat the whole thing like some amazing rain dancing opportunity. Make me laugh. But I wasn't here with Mason, I was here with Kevin. And that was okay — he deserved a chance too.

"Thank you for the ride." I smiled at the driver, then stepped into the rain.

There was no point in running — I was soaked almost immediately. My hair, my makeup, my clothes. It was all pointless — I probably looked like a drowned rat. I had to stifle a laugh. My first date, my best laid plans, all destroyed by a bit of weather in the first fifteen minutes. Life was unpredictable, it didn't really matter how much you prepared for it.

Kevin held the door open, his eyebrows raised. "You didn't run for it."

"Needed a shower," I said. "I had to wash off the inch of grime that's always covering me."

Kevin wrinkled his nose. "Gross."

I stepped past him, rolling my eyes. Apparently, Kevin didn't have a sense of humor. How had I not noticed that before? When you crushed on someone from a distance, you didn't notice their flaws. Just their virtues. Even a small crush could blind you to everything else. It was like paint hiding the cracks in a wall. But eventually the paint chipped off, and the cracks showed.

The cracks in Kevin's intellectual façade didn't disappear as we ate — instead they grew larger. When the waiter came, Kevin ordered for both of us before I could protest. He got my order wrong, too, and I had to chase the waiter down to tell him that no, I did not want cilantro on anything.

Then, while we were eating, Kevin talked the entire time about chess, board games, and strategy. He claimed that intelligence was knowing that there was a right course of action, and that he had a gift of always knowing what the right move was. That's why he was so good at chess. Apparently, he was playing some Russian grand master this week-end. Was he babbling nervously, like I used to, or did he just not care about anything I had to say? It was impossible to tell.

However, the worst offense came when the waiter guided us to the Smashing Room and gave us a plate to break to celebrate our first date in what the waiter assured us would be a long, amazing relationship.

Kevin held the plate in his hand, frowning. "I don't understand. Why are we supposed to break the plate?"

"Tradition," I said.

"It's stupid," Kevin replied. "Who breaks plates?"

I felt the urge to yank the plate from his hand. At least smashing something would add a slight thrill to this otherwise painfully boring first date.

"It's a waste, is all I'm saying," Kevin added. "It's not smart. Smashing a perfectly good plate is something a neanderthal would do. 'Oh hey, I'm a super tough man with plentiful muscles, and look at the thing I can break.' It's so stupid to just break something. But I guess those are the times we live in, aren't they? No one's impressed by a well-played game of chess, but everyone is impressed when some muscle head can kick a ball really far."

My misery was quickly turning to annoyance. Was Kevin always this pretentious? How had I not noticed? "It's just a plate," I said. "And you don't think sports requires any sort of intelligence? Ty always says football is like chess but athletic."

Kevin snorted. "That's the dumbest thing I ever heard. Sorry, I know he's your brother, but…"

"Yes. He is. And he's not dumb." I said. "Plus, Mason plays too."

As if Kevin didn't know this.

"Exactly," Kevin said. "And you saw me play him at chess. He wasn't even in the same league as me. I'm sure he's a nice enough guy — dumb guys usually are — but he's going to end up flipping burgers for his job. Or being a real estate agent."

I wondered if I'd get kicked out of Snack N' Smash for smashing a plate over Kevin's head. It was probably better if I didn't find out. "I have curfew," I said. "I need to go home."

"I have to break this stupid plate first." Kevin casually tossed the plate like a frisbee. It hit the wall with all the force of a feather. Best of all, it didn't break. It didn't even chip. "I thought these plates were supposed to be easy to break."

I shrugged. "Maybe if you played more sports, then you wouldn't—"

"I wouldn't what?" Kevin snapped, suddenly annoyed. "Throw like a girl?"

My blood boiled. I marched across the room, grabbed the plate, and hurled it against the wall.

It broke into a dozen pieces.

"Telling someone they throw like a girl isn't an insult." I glared at Kevin. "I'd rather throw like a girl than throw like you."

He shrugged. "If you won't be polite, you can find your own ride home. In the rain."

"I plan to."

44

ZOE

*T*he walk home from High Street was only fifteen minutes, but by the time I made it to my driveway, I was drenched. I stood alone, in the rain, in front of my house.

All the lights were off.

I tried to open the front door, but it was locked, and because Kevin rushed me to leave, I'd forgotten my house keys inside. My finger hovered over the doorbell.

So this was how my first date — my first real date — ended. With me, shivering and sad, standing in my doorway, begging to be let in.

This wasn't how dates were supposed to end. I hadn't practiced this.

Someone was home, and they'd answer the front door if I rang the doorbell. Would it be worse to bawl in front of Tyler or Mom? Tyler would probably threaten to beat up Kevin — jokingly — but that wasn't what I wanted. And Mom would tell me some stupid stat about how ninety percent of dates end like this. I didn't want either of them.

I wanted... Mason.

I wanted Mason more than anything in the world right now.

But that wasn't possible, so I wanted the next best thing: to be alone.

I went to the backyard, and in the rain, with my clothes soaked and clinging to me, I climbed into the treehouse. It was dark inside, almost pitch black.

Shivering, I stripped out of my dress and jacket and put them in a wet pile on the table.

Something crinkled.

I dug under the pile of clothes and found a bag sitting on the table. What was this? It was too dark to see, so I reached inside the bag and felt around.

My hand landed on something soft and fluffy.

I pulled it out.

It was a stuffed unicorn — practically a mirror image of Sparkles. It smelled like clean laundry and coconut sunscreen. Like Mason.

"Where did you come from?" My words trembled as they spilled from my lips. My eyes stung, and I suddenly felt very, very tired. Was I going to cry, or was I going to sleep? Or, more likely, was I going to cry myself to sleep with the mysterious unicorn?

I fought back tears as I climbed into one of the sleeping bags. Mason's, not mine. It still smelled like him, and when I wrapped myself up inside, it felt like I was getting the ghost of a hug from the boy I'd fallen for. As the tears threatened, I squeezed the stuffed unicorn tightly.

A recording of Mason's voice filled the treehouse. "What? How long does it record? Only fifteen seconds? Wait it started — oh no — Zoo! I picked this little guy up for you as a congrats for getting your first date. And a thank you for everything, I—"

The recording cut off.

The tears came.

As I lay in the darkness of the treehouse, the rain pounding against the roof, I squeezed the unicorn so many times that the battery wore out.

On the saddest night, in the October cold, it was a fifteen second snippet of Mason's voice that kept me warm.

45

MASON

*T*he next day was the Homecoming Dance, and High Street was bright and vibrant. Banners were strung between light posts, shop windows were painted in royal blue and gold, and there were bits of confetti on the asphalt from the morning's Homecoming parade. The rest of the football team and I all took part in the parade, walking down the center of the street and waving at everyone who came to support us.

Normally, the Homecoming parade — especially after a big win — was one of the highlights of the season. But today I wanted to skip it. I wanted to stay home, sleep, and try not to think about Zoe's date with Kevin.

After the parade, I took off my jersey, threw on a baseball cap and sunglasses, and wandered along High Street. I didn't feel like going home. I grabbed a hot dog from a cart that was set up along the parade route and ate while I walked. Part of me was dying to know how Zoe's date went, but I was determined not to text her. I didn't want to interfere.

I wandered the street, my head in a fog, and eventually arrived at the dance studio where I learned to two-step.

Memories flooded me. Zoe, in her cowboy hat, her hand on my shoulder, her eyes sparkling as she nimbly moved across the dance floor. I remembered laughing as she left, tipping her cowboy hat to a group of skaters as she moseyed down the street.

When I entered the dance studio, it was like walking back through time. The same seniors were two-stepping in a circle, the same country twang resounding through the space.

I tapped my feet to the rhythm and smiled. This was stupid. Why couldn't I tell Zoe how I felt? I pulled out my phone to text her, but before I could, Verity was on her way over.

"Looks like we caught a live one," she said, smiling. "You're back."

"I'm back."

"How about we have a dance?"

I shoved my phone back in my pocket. "Okay, but I have to warn you — there's a good chance I'll step on your toes."

"As long as you don't break my hip."

"I promise nothing."

Verity laughed.

We danced. I was extra careful to make sure I didn't step on her toes. I raised my arm, and she spun beneath.

"Zoe did a good job," Verity said. "You've spun me, you haven't stepped on my toes, and you haven't looked at your feet once. Not too shabby for someone who only started dancing a few weeks ago."

"I was lucky to have a great teacher," I said. That was true — Zoe was the best.

Verity smiled warmly. "I'm so happy that you two found each other."

"Oh, actually—"

Verity ignored my interruption. "You are quite a good

match. A dance can only be as good as the chemistry between the partners. And for these old eyes, you two have chemistry that's once-in-a-lifetime. And I would know — I've had a long lifetime."

I spun Verity again and swallowed. Hard. It felt like if I tried to correct her, she would bang me on the head and give me a stern talking to.

"If you don't mind me asking, dear, how did you invite her to the Homecoming Dance?"

And now there was no way out. "I, uh, I didn't."

Verity narrowed her eyes. "And why's that?"

I opened my mouth to say something, but realized there was nothing I could say.

"You look at me, dear," Verity said, her eyes ablaze. "That girl is special. And you're something special too. But if you want there to be something between the two of you, you're going to have to make a move. You can have all the kindling in the world, but if you don't strike a match, it'll never burn."

I was about to reply when my phone vibrated.

"Thank you for the dance," I said. "I have to take this."

"Think about what I said," Verity replied. "And don't let once in a lifetime pass you by."

She made her way back to the dance floor and found another partner.

That's how Zoe would be when she was older, I realized. Full of life, dancing up a storm. I wanted to be part of that life. I wanted to be part of Zoe's life. I checked the text on my phone.

It was from Tyler, and it only had five words:

Can we talk about Zoe?

46

ZOE

*T*he Homecoming dance was only a few hours away, and I was still curled in Mason's sleeping bag in the treehouse. I didn't want to move. I had just enough energy to put on my still-wet clothes, go to the house for breakfast (and a change into my pajamas), then immediately come back to the treehouse.

As far as I was concerned, the best way to get through Homecoming was to sleep through it. I told Ty I had no plans to go to the dance, and that I would be in the treehouse if he needed me. And that I'd prefer if he didn't need me.

I squeezed my stuffed unicorn.

Mason's voice echoed through the treehouse. "What? How long does it record? Only fifteen seconds? Wait it started — oh no — Zoo! I picked this little guy up for you as a congrats for getting your first date. And a thank you for everything, I—"

I, what? What was he going to say at the end of the recording?

I closed my eyes and tried to drift into what I hoped would be a dreamless sleep. I tried not to think about

180

Mason, about how he was probably getting ready for Homecoming right now. He'd have a corsage to give to Meredith when he picked her up. Then they'd go to the Homecoming Dance, and they'd win the competition, and be King and Queen, because of course they would. And I'd just be the average cliff note in his otherwise spectacular senior year.

The ladder to the treehouse creaked under someone's weight.

Mason? No. The thought was ridiculous. But as much as I tried to shut it down, I couldn't help but fantasize that the mystery person was Mason. That he'd come to take me to Homecoming, instead of Meredith.

Until he saw me. I hadn't washed the makeup off my face from last night. I was wearing old pajamas. And I hadn't showered. Or brushed my teeth. If it was Mason, he'd probably stick his head in the treehouse, then run screaming.

My mystery guest was not Mason.

It was Nina. She climbed in the treehouse, put her hands on her hips, and looked around, unimpressed. "You know you have a real home, right? With your very own bedroom, a kitchen, a bathroom… a shower. And… are you in Mason's sleeping bag right now?"

"Don't judge me." I held out the unicorn.

Nina gave it a squeeze.

The recording played.

She raised her eyebrows. "Well, that's adorable. And also makes me wonder — why are you still sitting here?"

I put the pillow over my face. "Because I don't want to go to Homecoming. And you can't make me."

"Why don't you want to go?"

Wasn't it obvious? I removed the pillow from my face. "Because he's going to be there with her. And they're going to dance. And win the stupid dance competition. And celebrate with a kiss, probably. My heart is barely intact as it is, you really want to risk all of that?"

Nina rubbed her eyes, looking very much like a band teacher fighting off a headache while trying to marshal her students through a challenging piece. "You're smart, Zoe. You really are. So why are you being so dumb?"

Normally, a shot like that would offend me. But today I didn't have the energy to be offended. "Because."

"You know Mason likes you." Nina stated it like it was an obvious, irrefutable fact. Like how the sky was blue, water was wet, and physics was the worst.

Hope sprang in my chest, but I quickly squashed it. Nothing could hurt your heart more than a little hope. "He doesn't like me. He was being nice."

Nina laughed. "Nice? He helped you throw a party. He took you on a 'fake' date — and turned this treehouse into a restaurant because you were grounded. He called me and asked about all of your favorite restaurants so he could make sure food you liked was on the menu. And he made you this." Nina squeezed the unicorn.

Mason's voice played.

She tossed the unicorn to me. "That's not something you do to be nice. He could've taught you how to date through email if he wanted to."

I played my trump card. "Then why is he going to Homecoming with Meredith?"

"Did you ask him to go to Homecoming?"

"No," I said. "And I'd point out that he didn't ask me either."

"Did you ever tell him you were interested?"

"No, and again—"

"Did you ever indicate that you might be interested?" Nina asked. "He literally told you how to show a guy you're interested, right? Get him alone, tell him about a place you're excited to go, lick his lips or whatever—"

"Look at his lips," I corrected. "And that was only for kissing."

Nina put her hands on her hips. "So? Did you do those things?"

"We were alone together," I said. "We danced together."

"And? Did you tell him about all the places you were excited to go?"

I frowned. I thought about all the signs I was supposed to give. All the little things I could do to show I was interested in someone. I hadn't done a single one of them to Mason. He literally gave me a playbook on how to show him I was interested — risk-free — and I hadn't given him any of the signals he would've looked for. "He still could've asked."

"Don't be difficult," Nina said. She sat beside me and looped her arm around my shoulders, giving me a comforting squeeze. "He told you everything you needed to do to show you were interested. And you didn't do any of those things. So he probably assumed you weren't interested."

Probably. Not that it helped me now.

Nina hugged me. "I'm proud of you. You put yourself out there to get a date with Kevin."

I gestured to the mess that was my current situation. "And that went so well."

"You tried. It didn't work out. You should still be proud because you tried," Nina said. "Think about it. At the start of the year, would you have actually gone for a boy if you liked them?"

I waited for her rant to continue. When it didn't, I asked, "is that a real question?"

"No," Nina said, answering her own question. "You

admired Kevin from afar, drooling at him from across the street."

"You make me sound super attractive."

Nina ignored me. "Even when the boy wasn't much of a prize. But Mason? Mason's a prize. And now you have a choice. You can either sit back and admire him from afar, watch as he lives his life, and yes, maybe gets together with Meredith. Or you can do something about it. I mean, how are you going to live with yourself if you don't at least put yourself out there?"

I could see the logic. But I was terrified of Mason in a whole different way than I was of Kevin. When things went poorly with Kevin, nothing bad actually happened. Like I didn't lose Kevin, I just never had him.

But Mason? If things went poorly, I could lose him forever. Years of friendship, childhood memories, perfect time spent together... all up in smoke. "What if I ruin what we have?"

Nina shrugged. "What if you spend the rest of your life wondering what could've been?"

Ugh. "Sometimes, I hate you," I said. "Especially those times when you're right."

"Like now?"

"Like now," I said. "Fine. I'll do it. I'll go to Homecoming. I'll cause a big scene."

"That's my girl." Nina squeezed me once more and wrinkled her nose. "But first, you need to shower."

47

ZOE

I climbed out of the backseat of our rideshare, hitching the long, silky skirt over my ankles to make sure it didn't get caught in the door. Mom and I had picked out this dress together months ago, and it had been hanging in my closet waiting for tonight. It was gorgeous — floor length, shimmery deep gold, with a sweetheart neckline and delicate spaghetti straps. For once, I felt beautiful.

Nina paid our driver and then hopped out of the car and twirled. She looked amazing herself, rocking a black ballerina dress with a poofy, tulle skirt. It was super unique, super Nina. I loved it.

And then I looked past Nina at the surrounding scenery.

"Are you out of your mind?" I asked.

"What are you talking about?"

"Um, everything?" I didn't know what kind of game she was playing, but we were nowhere near Beachbreak High. In fact, forest surrounded us in every direction. We were just on the edge of the trail that led to Highline Hideaway. "Homecoming is at school, unless something drastically changed in the last hour."

"Weird. Something must have changed." Nina winked and skipped past me. "Plus, I didn't say we were going to Beachbreak's Homecoming."

"Now you're just lying," I said. "I distinctly remember you saying I should go to Homecoming."

"And you are."

I could not have been more confused.

Nina grinned. "You're not going to Beachbreak's Homecoming. You're going to your Homecoming."

"What?"

Without another word, Nina turned down the trail. She pulled a small flashlight out of her purse and flashed the beam over the dirt path, pointing out any roots. Not that she needed to — I'd walked this path so many times I could probably do it with my eyes closed.

But I was still confused. And she STILL wasn't answering any of my questions. In fact, whenever I tried to get any information from her, she just said things like "interesting question" and "great observation" and "oh my goodness you talk a lot."

The trees broke, and a breath later, I was standing on Highline Hideaway.

For the first time in history, the beach was completely empty.

Except for one thing.

My inflatable unicorn, Sparkles, was sitting on the sand. Twinkling fairy lights were looped around his neck and horn. It was like he was waiting for me.

"Nina," I said, my mouth suddenly dry. "What's—"

"Go look."

My stomach was a tangle of nervous knots. I slipped off my shoes and let them dangle by my side as I walked across the cool sand. The closer I got to Sparkles, the more my hopes rose. I tried to stay calm, to keep my heart in check, but it was like trying to force a lid on a boiling pot. No matter how hard you shoved the lid down, pressure built up and pushed it off. "Don't get your hopes up," I muttered.

Sparkles smiled at me. There was a bottle on his back. It looked like there was something inside the bottle. Something that looked a lot like a message.

Despite the warmth of the evening, it was getting difficult to breathe. My chest rose and fell and my hands trembled as I reached for the bottle. After a moment of struggle, I pulled off the cork. There was a loud popping sound.

I turned the bottle upside down and shook out the message.

It fell to the sand.

I picked it up. Unraveled it.

Mason's handwriting.

You know the place. M.

"What's it say?" Nina asked.

I jumped. "Way to sneak up on me."

Nina looked at the note eagerly. "What's it say?"

"He wants me to meet him at our cove." I glanced from Nina to Sparkles. I would need to take the unicorn to get there, and there was a very real risk of ruining my dress. Not that I'd ever been one for fancy dresses. "If I go, I need to take Sparkles."

"If?"

There was a lump in my throat. "What if it doesn't work out?"

48

MASON

*W*aiting on the beach made me as nervous as every big football game I'd played put together. It was my own personal Super Bowl, the most important game of my life. Except this wasn't a game. It wasn't practice. This was the real thing.

If she came.

I adjusted the collar of my dress shirt and straightened the cuffs on my jacket. I held a corsage in my hand, a single deep red rose — beautiful and classy, like Zoe herself. I was wearing a navy-blue suit, and to be honest, it probably looked a little ridiculous because I didn't have shoes or socks on. Dress shoes were uncomfortable.

I paced across Secret Cove. Earlier in the day, Ty had called me. Actually called me, not just texted. He wanted to talk to me about Zoe. Apparently, her date with Kevin hadn't gone well, and she was completely miserable. The idea that her first date was a disaster broke my heart. I wanted her to be happy, even if she wasn't with me, and I told Ty as much. Then he told me that the happiest he had seen her was when she was with me.

And then I told him everything I'd been feeling, how I had fallen for Zoe without ever planning to. How spending time with her had made me see something that had been right there, in front of me, for most of my life. I told him that Zoe had my heart. All of it.

And then I asked if I could ask out his sister.

"You don't need my permission, dude," Ty said. "All that matters is what she wants."

"Do you know what she wants?"

"Nope," Tyler said. "That's for you to find out. I promise nothing."

And then, after helping me set up, Tyler was off, on his own date to Homecoming with Parker. And me... I was still waiting.

The wind picked up, a warm October breeze.

My phone buzzed. A message from Meredith. She said everything was okay, that I clearly liked Zoe, and that she hoped I got her. I thanked her for her message and apologized again.

Then it was back to waiting.

My nervousness was getting worse. And why wouldn't it? Waiting for something to happen was always the worst — or best, depending on how it turned out. Being in the locker room before the game started was more nerve-wracking than being on the field. I took a deep breath and looked up.

There was something coming around the bend.

Something bright.

Lights reflected off the water.

And past that reflection was a floating unicorn with the most beautiful girl in the world.

49

ZOE

*I*n my life, I have never been more awkward than when I was lying on an inflatable unicorn in my Homecoming dress, trying to paddle Sparkles around the bend to Secret Cove. I was probably the most ridiculous thing in the Pacific Ocean that night. And I was probably completely wrecking my dress, thanks to the steady spray of salt water. But I needed to know what was around the bend.

Then I saw it.

And I lost my breath.

Secret Cove was decorated like something out of a dream. Two strands of fairy lights climbed the palm trees on either side of the hammock, and tiki torches marked the shoreline. There was a picnic blanket with plates of food and a cooler of drinks. Above the blanket, stretched between two trees, was a banner announcing Homecoming King and Queen.

But there was something better than all the incredible decorations: Mason.

He was standing barefoot in the sand, wearing a navy-blue suit that made his eyes glow sapphire. His beautiful face was lit up by the sparkling fairy lights. He was smiling.

For the umpteenth time in the last twenty-four hours, I wanted to cry. But this time it wasn't from sadness or pity. I rubbed the tears from my eyes, mildly agitated that they were blurring my view. I paddled as hard as I could, completely ignoring the cold ocean water soaking the hem of my dress. I needed to get to the cove. I needed to get to Mason.

He kneeled, rolled up his pant legs, and came out into the surf. Without a word, he grabbed Sparkles, and pulled the unicorn — and me — onto the sand.

I felt like there was a giant lump stuck in my throat. What was I supposed to say? What could I say? I climbed off Sparkles and stared at the beach, our own private Homecoming. But why?

Mason tapped his phone and music played from hidden speakers.

A waltz.

He inclined his head slightly and extended his hand. "Zoe Walsh, will you be my date to Homecoming?"

There were so many butterflies fluttering around my stomach that I was worried I'd open my mouth and one would fly out. So, instead of speaking, I nodded.

I took his hand, and he pulled me close. He leaned forward, resting his forehead against mine. When he spoke, his voice was low and breathy. "In that case, may I have this dance?"

We waltzed across the beach, staring into each other's eyes. Mason danced with confidence, not needing to look at his feet anymore.

He bit his lip. "I spent the last two hours rehearsing a speech, but one look at you and I can't remember what I was going to say."

My cheeks burned red and my heart skipped a beat. I smiled. "Try?"

191

We did a perfect outside spin, his eyes still on mine. "You are the most beautiful, most amazing person I've ever met. My cheeks hurt for hours after we're together because I've been laughing so hard. And when I'm with you, all I want to do is stay awake because you're better than anything I could dream."

My heart melted like ice cream on a summer day. My legs must've melted too, because I missed the next step in the waltz and almost brought us both down.

But Mason caught me, adjusted our rhythm, and kept dancing like nothing had gone wrong.

Wow. My brother's best friend, the hot quarterback who could make me laugh like no one else, and now he knew how to dance, too? It wasn't possible for him to get better. But, while these things about Mason were amazing, none of them were what truly mattered. Mason could be terrible at sports and have two left feet and I would still be head over heels for him. For who he was.

Mason was smart, funny, warm, caring, and kind. And I didn't want anyone but him.

I still couldn't find the words I wanted, so I just fell into his eyes and continued to dance.

"And there's one other thing," Mason said.

I held my breath.

He stared deeply into my eyes. "I'm falling in love with you."

If words were difficult to come by before, they were impossible now. But maybe I didn't need words to express how I felt. I did the only thing I could think of: I glanced at his lips, then back at his eyes.

Mason brushed the hair from my face, and we stopped dancing. He gently pulled my chin up towards him.

Warmth rushed over my body, and my arms and legs tingled with anticipation. I felt his body against mine, my chest against his. He smelled clean and warm, aftershave mingling with sea salt. In that moment, all I wanted was him.

His lips met mine.

Soft.

Confident.

Perfect.

He could hold my body against his forever and it still wouldn't be long enough.

I looped my arms around his neck and kissed him back passionately. Then I pulled back ever so slightly, and with our noses still touching, I whispered. "I'm in love with you too."

He kissed me again.

Then we pulled apart.

"Thank you for the unicorn," I said, smiling. "I love it."

"You should've seen me trying to get the recording right. Had a heck of a time." Mason laughed. Then he gestured to the picnic blanket. "I've prepared a small Homecoming feast for us. Complete with—"

He grabbed two ridiculous plastic crowns from the picnic blanket. He set one on my head.

I took the second crown and placed it on his head. "We're practically royalty now. Does this mean we get to feast like royalty, too?"

"You know it," Mason said. He unveiled the meal. We had the same burgers and fries we had at the Treehouse Café. There were also several bowls of snacks — popcorn and candy — from the night of our impromptu sleepover. And in the cooler? Churro sundaes.

"The Treehouse Café's expanding," I said. "And I commend you on your food choices."

He held my hand as I sat. "Do you recognize anything else?"

I looked at the food and the blanket. But there was nothing I recognized. I frowned. "I'm missing something?"

He tapped my plate.

It was a regular, white plate, except it was creased with random lines of gold. I picked it up to examine it, tracing my fingers along the sparkling lines.

"They're also from the Treehouse Café," Mason said. "I found a place that could put them back together."

I looked at his plate. Sure enough, there was only a single gold line on it from where it had split in half from his tremendously awkward throw. "Why?"

"Because it was the best date of my life," Mason said. "And when you have a date that spectacular, you need to keep something to remember it."

I clutched the plate to my chest. "I'm keeping one."

He grinned. "That was the plan."

We ate, we chatted, we laughed, we danced, and yes, we kissed. I couldn't believe how anyone could get as lucky as me. All of my time spent admiring boys from afar, and the first boy I fell for, the first boy I truly loved, was the one who was closest to me. My brother's best friend.

After everything we'd been through and experienced together, there was only one boy for me.

In the end, it had to be Mason.

50

ZOE

*M*ason and I were only two weeks into our official relationship, but two weeks of being Mason's — official — girlfriend were amazing. We ate our lunches together in the cafeteria, and we continued to work on our Life Skills project. Sometimes, Mason got us out of class. And sometimes, when we were out of class, we actually worked on our Life Skills project.

The end of football season was still a few weeks away, but Mason and I decided that when it was over, we'd sign up for a swing dance class on High Street. Mason's idea, not mine. He'd fully accepted the dancer inside of himself, and even though the guys on the football team started calling him "Twinkle Toes," he told me he thought the nickname was hilarious — and he kind of liked it. He said it was like naming a big dog "Fluffy."

"You're daydreaming again, aren't you?" Nina asked.

Her voice snapped me back to reality. "Guilty," I said.

It was Saturday morning, the morning of Halloween. Nina was in my kitchen sorting through a bowl of candy. "Since we're too old to Trick or Treat, we should just take the candy we want now. Your mom always buys too much anyway."

"I heard that," Mom shouted from her office.

"What I mean to say is thank you!" Nina shouted back.

Mom laughed.

I laughed too. "Honestly, we're both short enough that if we dressed in the right costumes, we could still get candy."

"Not with him you can't," Nina said, pointing her thumb at Mason.

He held his hand over his heart and feigned hurt. "You could get candy with me. I'll have you know that I'm barely more mature than a child."

We both laughed.

Mason grinned. "And now this kid has to go get his costume ready." He took off upstairs.

"Will you two be at High Street tonight?" Nina asked.

I was practically vibrating with excitement. "Not only will we be at the Haunting at High Street, we're going to the dance studio to learn the Thriller dance first. Then, when the song hits on the speakers, we're going to do it in the middle of the street. You should come."

"I want to, but…" Nina examined a piece of candy, weighed it, then tossed it in her personal pile.

"But what?"

"I'm really happy you're happy, Zoe. I am. Like, so very, very happy." She sighed. "But I'm also jealous. You haven't left me out or anything, I just wish I had a boyfriend that I could do all the cute couchley stuff with. You know?"

I knew exactly how she felt. Two months ago, I would've thought it was impossible for me to get a boyfriend. I squeezed my friend's hand. "You'll get there. Now that I know what I'm doing, maybe I can teach you a few tricks."

"You better," Nina said, grinning. "And you better do it soon. Christmas is right around the corner, and I would very much like to have someone to take me to all the Christmas Candy Canes that pop up around Beachbreak. If I don't have a boyfriend by then, I might just have to fake it."

I laughed. "I'm sure it won't come to that."

Nina tore open a caramel and popped it in her mouth. "Can you imagine? Me with a fake boyfriend?"

Just as she finished speaking, Tyler popped in the kitchen. Half of his body was wrapped in toilet paper and safety pins. He was trying, and failing, to be a cursed Egyptian mummy.

"You look ridiculous." I told him.

"Wait 'til you see your boyfriend." He laughed. Boyfriend. It still felt strange hearing that word — especially out of my big brother's mouth. But Tyler had been amazing about Mason and I getting together. He even told me if his little sister had to date anyone, he would prefer it to be someone he actually liked and respected. It made me even more thankful than usual to have a brother like him.

Tyler's eyes zeroed in on Nina's pile of candy. He reached for a caramel.

She swatted his hand. "You're too old for Halloween candy."

"Dude, I'm literally one year older than you."

"Which makes you one year too old for Halloween candy." Nina said.

"But you're taking all the best ones," Tyler replied. "Those are literally all of my favorites."

Nina shrugged. "What can I say? I have excellent taste. You can't blame me for that."

My brother stalked away. He stopped in the doorway, turned to us, and shook his fist comically.

"I'll get you for this, Nina, if it's the last thing I do." He howled in a stupid, spooky voice.

She rolled her eyes and pelted him with a caramel.

ZOE

I rested my hand on Mason's shoulder as we walked to High Street on Halloween night. Kids ran from house to house, screaming and laughing, collecting so much candy that their teeth would probably rot overnight. Not that we were any better — Mason and I had stuffed our costumes with as much candy as they could hold.

It felt like the night had limitless possibilities.

I also felt something else.

Contentment.

Happiness.

When I was with Mason, it felt like nothing could go wrong. It felt like I fit perfectly into his life. With his arm around my shoulder, things just felt… right.

"I still can't believe you pulled off our own private Homecoming," I said. "You're a genius."

Mason blushed.

Like, he actually blushed.

"Oh my goodness." I pointed at his cheeks. "Look at you. You're turning red."

"I am not," he said, swatting my finger away. "It's Halloween makeup."

"Oh, it's definitely not." I grinned wickedly. "I made you blush! I made you blush! I made you—"

He silenced me with a kiss. When our lips finally broke apart, he was smiling.

I waited for my breath to return. "I hope you know you can't just kiss me every time you want to get away with something."

He winked. "We'll see."

I squeezed his hand, and we continued our trek towards High Street. "So. Ready to do some more dancing, Space Face?"

He returned my squeeze. "As long as you're with me, Zoo, I'm ready for anything."

Thank you so much for reading!

If you enjoyed this book, please leave me a review. As a new author, reviews mean everything to me. I appreciate each and every one of them.

Printed in Great Britain
by Amazon

78186289R10120